If This Was a Game,
I Didn't Want to Play

Back and forth we went, two hundred pounds of St. Bernard making the hundred-yard dash around the pool, and mighty Mrs. Mouse scrambling the seventeen feet across the plastic that covered it. Something had to give.

Mrs. Mouse stood on her haunches in the middle of the pool, squeaking mouse taunts. The cactus she had been hoarding fell out of her mouth.

When she ducked to reclaim it, one of the stickers caught in the plastic.

I galloped to the diving board and reached my paw over the water. But then the board began to bend....

When the board dipped, so did I. Though my paw bounced Mrs. Mouse clear across the plastic, my claws got caught on the return swing.

I tried to shake my paw loose, but the diving board shuddered under my weight.

Boing. Boing. Boing.

I held on.

BOOIING.

It was one too many.

Splash.

The cannonball could have made the Guinness Book of World Records.

The plastic was sinking, and unless I got it off my paw, I'd be keeping it company.

Judge Benjamin: The Superdog Rescue

Judith Whitelock McInerney

Illustrated by Leslie Morrill

PUBLISHED BY
SIMON & SCHUSTER, INC.

for KELLY—
my cheerleader and friend

 A MINSTREL BOOK, published by
Simon & Schuster, Inc., 1230 Avenue
of the Americas, New York, N.Y. 10020

Copyright © 1984 by Judith Whitelock McInerney
Illustrations copyright © 1984 by Leslie Morrill
Cover artwork copyright © 1986 by Richard Williams

Published by arrangement with Holiday House
Library of Congress Catalog Card Number: 83-48961

ISBN: 0-671-64067-4

First Minstrel Books printing November, 1986

First special printing December, 1986

10 9 8 7 6 5 4 3 2 1

A MINSTREL BOOK and colophon are trademarks of Simon & Schuster, Inc.

Printed in the U.S.A.

Chapter 1

A soothing rain pattered on the awning of the Pace Arrow camper our first early morning back in Decatur, Illinois.

I listened to it for nearly an hour before the children began to stir. It had been so late when we pulled into our driveway the night before that Maggie and Tom O'Riley had let the children finish sleeping in the vacation camper. Tom and Maggie, anxious to see the remodeling work that had been in progress when we left, had spent the night in the big house.

I wanted to see it, too. But someone needed to stay with the kids, and I didn't mind.

Judge Benjamin O'Riley—that's what they call me.

Not a Supreme Court justice, mind you, just a family St. Bernard with four special children to watch over.

Kathleen pulled back the curtains in the camper with a yawn, shaking her mussed braids. "We're home, guys."

Seth grunted an answer but he didn't get up. He was getting old enough to appreciate sleeping in.

Annie Elizabeth banged the screen door on her way out to my spot by the camper. She brought me one of her best good-morning hugs. Annie would be having a fourth birthday soon.

"Judge! Whyn't you tell us? We's home!" she squealed.

I shrugged apologetically.

It was enough. Annie gave me a forgiving smile and patted my nose.

"Annie, come get your shoes on if you're going up to the big house," Kathleen said. She was holding a sleepy Maura and fastening her sandals. It was quite a trick since Maura had a firm grip on Kathleen's braids.

Seth finally gave in to the noise and jumped from his bunk. "I can't put up with three sisters in this weakened condition. Let's go eat."

Seth and I definitely understood one another.

He rubbed my ears, and we led the way to the house.

Maggie and Tom were waving from the doorway.

"C'mon, kids. We thought you'd never wake up," Maggie said. "I almost couldn't keep your dad from eating all the biscuits and honey."

Biscuits and honey? Now I knew we were home.

The smell of Maggie's warm baking-powder rolls wasn't the only surprise waiting for us. The house had never looked so beautiful.

When we had last seen it, it was in a state of disrepair from the ravages of an April tornado. Our trip in the Pace Arrow camper had been, in part, a way to avoid the noise and mess of construction.

It wasn't as good as before—it was better.

What had already been a special home now seemed brighter and fresher.

We went off in separate directions, all of us checking our most loved spots. In my corner by the kitchen's Dutch door, a thick, rusty-toned rug covered most of the shiny vinyl floor. There was enough acrylic softness for all of my two hundred pounds. I heard Annie squealing about a new dollhouse she'd discovered in the room she now shared with Kathleen. Seth and Kathleen were cheering about a new game table.

But the biggest marvel was for all of us.

"Go ahead, Maggie. You do the honors," Tom said.

I could smell the chlorine as soon as Maggie slid the wide tempered doors into a wall pocket. Just off the dining room, where the table had been set with a linen tablecloth, brassware, and china, a great new room addition greeted us. It had redwood walls, tall wind-out windows, and a huge fireplace that blended beautifully with the rest of the house. But—there was more. Three steps down from a redwood deck was a swimming pool!

"Is it real?" The question came from Kathleen, but it was Annie who marched to the water's edge, removed her shoe and sock, and tested.

"Yup. It's real water."

Seth was beside her. "You better be careful, Annie. How deep is it, Mom?"

"Nine and a half feet at the far end down there." Maggie pointed. "But it only goes to four feet at the rope, so there is some leeway at this side for Annie to learn to swim."

"I cin swim. See?"

Never mind that she was wearing clothes. Forget that we were all close enough to block her dive. Dear Annie managed to plunge in anyway.

A cold splash of water found my nose.

Another spatter skimmed my eyeballs.

I mean, it was really *cold*.

In the time I blinked, Tom stepped in, shoes and all, and fished out a coughing, sputtering girl. "I'm fine, Daddy. I coulda made it out."

"No, Annie, we're going to set some rules now, and you're going to understand. Or you won't taste a Twinkie for two months!"

Twinkie? He would take away her Twinkies?

Tom took off his loafers and dumped water within inches of my paw. "A little slow on the uptake, huh, pal?" He was smiling, but I felt guilty. I should have been the one to move fast and pull Annie out.

I could see my Twinkies fading into the sunset, too.

A knot tightened in my chest. A swimming pool meant a new responsibility for the family Saint. Even though I wasn't about to lather myself with suntan oil, outfit myself with Foster Grant sunglasses and a whistle, and park myself in a chair that read LIFEGUARD, I intended to get my swimming act together anyway.

Chapter 2

The rules were simple enough for everyone to understand.

Annie could not go near the pool without Tom or Maggie. The dining room doors were to be kept locked because of Maura. No one was to swim alone, and no one was allowed near the pool fully dressed. Seth proved the need for the last rule when he fell in while counting the tiles by footsteps around the edge of the pool.

Tom put a little stool by the dining room doorway and taught Annie how to manage the locks. After locking the big slider, Annie was instructed to give the key back to Tom or Maggie. By giving her such an important job, they knew she'd remember the rules.

For the swim frolics that afternoon, I managed to stay out of the way of the biggest splashes. I hugged a corner by the fireplace and the life preservers, but I knew it was just a matter of time till I got into the act for real. If those kids needed me, I had to be ready.

When the sun finally went down on our first day back in the new-old home, I dragged my rug to the spot by the life preservers.

"You really like our new pool, don't you, big fella?" Tom patted my head and smiled.

I felt like a hypocrite, but maybe I *would* learn to like it. I took a little drink from the corner at the deep end. It didn't seem quite so cold now, just pleasantly cool.

"Okay, it's fine with me," Tom said. "I don't blame you a bit. Actually it's nice and cool now with these windows open."

Tom found a length of Visqueen to cover the pool. It was a clean, clear plastic, the kind he used in his construction work when he enclosed temporary openings. He reasoned that it would keep the water clean while cutting down on the evaporation that could cause too much humidity in the house. He and Seth pulled it over the water and cut it to fit the sides, leaving a slight overlap around the edges. The blue water flickered beneath it, and unless you stood right over it, it was hard to tell that it was covered at all.

After saying prayers with the children, Maggie and Tom came out one more time. They didn't say anything, just stood together and took in the new room—the plants Grammy had sent that gave the room a tropical air, the bamboo rockers at the north end, the clean white diving board.

Annie called for Maggie, and Tom stayed behind an extra minute to close the damper on the fireplace. Then he patted my head and left.

I could feel some of my anxiety slipping away. I studied the water and the room, and made every effort to pump my brain with positive thinking.

That's when I had my first visitor.

The house was incredibly quiet. No doubt the whole family had gone right to sleep.

A little bump of gray fur peeked around the Scotch pine tree in the redwood planter on the left side of the fireplace.

Uh-oh.

With all the construction—the open doors, the workers coming and going—a mouse had moved in.

He was joined by what had to be his wife.

She didn't peek, she darted—straight for the cactus, where she hopped on the clay pot and began chewing.

Wouldn't that hurt? All those thistles?

But it didn't seem to bother her. She held a big chunk in her cheek and darted back to a spot behind the Scotch pine. When she came back again, her cheek was empty.

Hmmm. Something told me there were probably junior mice.

Mr. Mouse was still peeking. He sidled up to the coleus and pulled off a leaf.

Mrs. Mouse was back at the cactus.

This was not good and I knew it. If I didn't act, I was liable to be replaced by a thin Siamese who could convince the unwanted tenants to go elsewhere. Maggie would not share her house with the uninvited.

I stood up and growled.

Mr. Mouse disappeared behind the Scotch pine.

Mrs. Mouse could have cared less.

She was packing more little bites of the cactus into her mouth.

Hmmph. I'd show her.

I pushed out my chest to lion fullness and took one step.

She looked up but went right back to her chore.

Looked up? Didn't flinch?

Was I losing my touch?

I marched toward her.

That did it. She finally moved away. But she didn't go back to the Scotch pine. She spotted the coleus that Mr. Mouse had been nibbling on and headed for that. She got there by walking across the Visqueen.

The nerve!

I went around the pool and met her on the other side.

I swear she smiled. Then she squeaked something in mouse talk. It was just as well I didn't understand the language. She scampered back across the Visqueen to the cactus.

If this was a game, I didn't want to play.

Back and forth we went, two hundred pounds of St. Bernard making the hundred-yard dash around the pool and mighty Mrs. Mouse scrambling the seventeen feet across it.

Something had to give. This peewee mouse who wasn't afraid to walk on water shouldn't have been able to outmaneuver an enemy the size of Moby Dick.

Mrs. Mouse got cocky, and that was a fatal

mistake. She stood on her haunches in the middle of the pool, squeaking mouse taunts. The cactus she had been hoarding fell out of her mouth.

When she ducked to reclaim it, one of the stickers caught in the Visqueen. It stuck.

It was my turn to snicker.

I saw my opportunity.

I galloped to the diving board and reached my paw over the water. I only needed to scare her into setting up housekeeping somewhere else. But when I lifted my paw and took the swing, the diving board began to bend. . . .

It must have been all those biscuits and honey. When the board dipped, so did I. Though my paw bounced Mrs. Mouse clear across the Visqueen, my claws got caught in the plastic on the return swing.

I tried to shake my paw loose, but the diving board shuddered under my weight.

Boing.

Boing. Boing. Boing.

I held on.

Up.

Down.

BOOIING.

It was one too many.

Splash.

The cannonball could have made the *Guinness Book of World Records.*

I couldn't believe no one heard it. It must have been the triple thermal glass doors.

The Visqueen was sinking, and unless I got it off my paw, I'd be keeping it company.

Perhaps if I rode it to the bottom of the pool, the weight of the water would pull it away from me and I could swim to the surface.

It was a good idea, but it took more seconds than I thought I had air.

At the nine-foot mark I bobbed, holding my breath and pushing the plastic off my paws.

I almost managed, until the Visqueen hooked to the drain and pulled it from its moorings.

The drain plug had lodged against the plastic, and the water was going out.

Gurgle, gurgle.

Now I had sound effects.

Ah, doom.

But at least the whirlpool of draining water began to pull the Visqueen away from my body. I fought my way through the swirls to the top of the pool.

It was all I could do to tread water and breathe.

In a surge of adrenaline brought on by sheer fear, I managed one thundering *WOOF!* between glugs.

It was more effective than the cannonball. St. Bernard sounds must penetrate glass.

In seconds Maggie and Tom appeared, barefoot and sleepy.

Tom unlocked the door but dropped the keys. While he fumbled around, trying to pick them up, Maggie charged in ahead of him. She walked right by the Scotch pine and stepped on Mrs. Mouse's tail.

Maggie looked down at the gray pointy tail poking through her toes, then she looked at me floundering in the bottom of the pool, and then —she did a most unliberated thing.

She screamed.

What was worse, Maggie was so stunned by the furry, squirming tail beneath her that she just stood there, frozen by indecision.

By this time the water had drained completely out.

I tried to climb to the shallow end, but I kept slipping, first on the tangled plastic and then on the pool's slick fiberglass.

Four saviors in pajamas suddenly appeared.

Annie threw me all the life preservers—a genius plan, since there was no longer any water.

Seth sat down by his father and laughed.

Big macho heroes, those guys.

But calm, clear-headed Kathleen, carrying Maura, was all business. She took a deep breath and handed Maura to her dad. Then Kathleen walked over to her mother, lifted Maggie's foot, grabbed the mouse by the tail, opened the back door, pitched the problem into the bushes, and brushed her palms with satisfaction.

Feminists everywhere would have been proud.

Until she fainted.

Seth stopped laughing long enough to catch her.

Chapter 3

We never saw the mice again. The mouse family must have spread the word that the house was full of crazies with their own Loch Ness monster.

As for me, I learned to love the pool. I knew better than to wear out my welcome or Tom would be cleaning filters forever. With my confidence restored after the mouse ordeal, I took my turn swimming with the family. Maura bounced around in floaties, and I gave rides to Annie. Seth and Kathleen and I had races. Once when Tom was floating on a rubber raft reading the Sunday paper, Maggie and the kids got me to upset his comfy spot.

Boy, did we laugh.

The sounds of lapping water and the echoes of Maura's blowing bubbles—well, the pool nearly always meant having special times together.

Tom was gone a lot. He'd taken over the camper as a job trailer. The driveway seemed a little bare at first, but we got used to it.

We were having such a good summer. But when I saw the apples plumping out on our trees, I knew our lazy days were coming to an end.

"Seth, you're supposed to write three book reports before school starts. Sister Mary Clare said at least three, and here it is ten days till we register and you can't even find a pencil!" Seth ignored Kathleen's scolding, but she went on, "I mean it, Seth, if Mom knew . . ."

Maggie picked that moment to walk into the kitchen, where we were sitting, and suddenly, Mom knew.

Seth found his pencil. By the time the bus honked on the first day of school, he'd finished *five* unsmudged papers that Sister Mary Clare could be proud of. Kathleen, in her neatly pressed uniform, counted them three times in disbelief.

While Kathleen and Seth were at school, Maura and Annie and I spent a lot of time on the patio and under the apple trees. September is a good month in Decatur. It's sweater weather early in the morning and late in the evening, but at midday the sun is warm and the air is crisp.

With Annie's careful coaching and with the help of my thick fur, Maura began pulling herself up. It was easy for her to grab hold, and I didn't mind.

The apples got bigger, and the limbs, heavy with their load, hung lower. There was barely room for Maura to crawl under them.

By the first week in October, it was picking time.

Maggie started things rolling with a hearty breakfast cooked outside. She liked fall mornings as much as I did.

Tom got up early and started the coals on the grill. While the family grabbed another half-hour of shut-eye, he read the paper.

I jogged some to make room for the eggs and sausages and pancakes that I knew would tempt me beyond the limits of a fair morning calorie count.

When I came back to the final smells of the cooking, Maggie and Seth were setting the table. "Tom, could you get Maura's highchair? She'll never sit still out here without it," Maggie said.

"Cin I hab juzz and milk, Mom? I'm really thirzdy." Annie's wish was granted. Before we all sat down, she'd taken a sip of each and spilled the rest.

"Is there any more of that blueberry syrup Grammy made?" Seth asked.

"Seth, you ate it all two days after Christmas, and you've asked that question every time we've had pancakes since," Kathleen pointed out.

"Well, maybe she sent some more." Seth was always hoping.

I could hardly blame him. That was Seth's all-time favorite pig-out food, and I had to agree that Grammy's homemade syrup was a ten.

"I don't know what we're going to do with all these apples, Maggie. You could bake every day for a month and still have loads." Tom was passing up seconds on sausage.

I loved it when he was dieting. It meant Fullsville for me.

"I've been thinking about that. It really is the biggest harvest we've had," Maggie said. "And it's such a beautiful time of year for a drive. Why don't we take a trunkful down to Metropolis to Grammy and Pa? We can give a few to Aunt Phyllis and Great-Gramps. . . ."

"Aunt Phyllis who always brings those expensive chocolates?" Seth stopped eating his eleventh pancake long enough to ask.

That boy was amazing. With his appetite, I suspected he was part St. Bernard.

"Great-Gramps? With the magic hand?" Annie asked.

"It's not magic, Annie," Kathleen said.

"'Tis too."

"It's artificial but it works on muscle impulses," Maggie explained. "And I'm inclined to agree with Annie that that is magical indeed."

Annie looked quite pleased with herself.

"Are we going to miss school?" It was Seth, naturally.

"Mom's talking about a weekend trip," Kathleen broke in. "You are talking about a weekend trip, aren't you, Mom? We have a big spelling bee coming up and . . ."

Kathleen's top bureau drawer was filled with holy cards she'd won since her first second-grade spelling competition.

"Of course, a weekend trip. I've enjoyed being home so much lately, I don't think I want to spend more than a couple of days away either!" Maggie said. "How many bushels can we fit in the station wagon with the seven of us?"

I was glad she said seven. My heart always

missed a beat until the plans were definite.

While Tom and Maggie discussed the apple arithmetic, Maura began a counting system of her own. Take one bite from one pancake, toss two to the Judge. Take one bite from another pancake, toss three to the Judge.

No one seemed to notice that the supply on the platter was thinning out.

Nice game.

The bright red station wagon was fun for short trips. It had replaced the Gremlin after Maura was born. Since the camper was on a Wisconsin job site, the station wagon would have to be roomy enough.

"We'll squeeze in as many bushels and boxes as we can," Tom was saying. "If word spreads through the family that we have free apples to hand out, we may meet a lot more Metropolis relatives than we know we have."

Maggie and Tom both laughed.

I recognized the signs. A family gathering was happening at the drop of an apple.

Maggie went into the house with a load of dishes, and when she came out, she announced she'd confirmed the get-together with Grammy, long distance.

"We're going to meet at Great-Gramps's farm," she said, passing empty boxes to the kids.

"You can each have your own tree. Start at the bottom and work your way up. Dad and I will get the top branches with the apple picker."

"That's one way of making sure Great-Gramps will be there," Tom said, hoisting the long wooden handle of the apple picker to the top of the Jonathan tree. It took mere seconds for him to snap an apple into the mesh caging and drop it down to Maggie. "Remember when he bought us this tool? I think it was the last time he took any time away from the farm."

"But he loves that farm, Dad." Kathleen's box was filled the fastest, and she didn't stop working when she started talking. "Sometimes I think he likes cows and chickens better than people."

"And horses," Seth put in. "Remember, he boards horses for some of the townies."

The word *horse* must have had some special meaning for Maura. She stopped playing with her music blocks and crawled toward me to pull herself up. Since I was lying down, she swung her leg over my back and started rocking.

Annie had gone to the farthest Golden Delicious tree and perched herself on a branch, examining each apple carefully for worms before she permitted it a treasured spot in her picking pail.

"It's his whole life now that Lula's gone," Maggie explained. "They worked that farm together for so many years that I guess it's a little like . . . oh, I don't know. Maybe you should ask Great-Gramps some time why he works so hard."

Great-Gramps was one of my favorite people. The freak accident with the combine that injured his hand had changed his appearance but not his attitude. He worked hard without complaining. And when his wife, Lula, had had an unexpected stroke, he'd accepted her death without bitterness, too.

Tom was filling basket number two. "Great-Gramps told me once that even though he knew Lula was gone, he could feel her like a shadow everywhere on the farm."

"Great-Gramps doesn't say much, but when he does, it's usually something important like that," Kathleen added matter-of-factly.

Annie jumped from her perch and stood where it was sunny, trying to examine her shadow. I thought she'd ask Maggie another deep, philosophical, three-year-old question, but apparently Annie was satisfied.

The conversation tapered off. I suppose everyone had been given something to think about.

Except Maura, whose ride-'em-cowboy game

had gotten old. She was ready for some acrobatics.

The tiny toes that had hugged my sides were scooting into a higher position. I could tell from her shifting weight that she had found a new lever to pull herself up with.

An apple branch.

I kept hoping someone would see her.

She was standing on my back now.

I stood up very slowly. I didn't dare let her suspend herself.

I wanted to bark, but I was afraid I'd frighten her and she would fall.

I had to do something.

I knew she was going higher.

A sparrow chirped nearby and gave me an idea.

But of course. I would sing.

From deep in my throat, I combined a perfectly respectable bass howl with a hum of considerable variety.

The O'Rileys raced en masse to Maura's rescue.

Chapter 4

Even after Seth and I delivered two bushels of apples to the Lockleys and Tom took two to the convent and the rectory, we had three times as many apples as we had room for in the car. So during the week before we left, Seth and Kathleen peeled, Annie washed, and Maggie baked—forty-two apple pies.

My job was sniff timer.

I could tell exactly when the crusts turned golden and when the cinnamon and sugar soaked into perfectly tender apples. I stood in front of the oven seconds before the automatic timer went off, every time.

With me, nothing ever overbaked.

Only thirty-six pies made it through the week, though. Maggie blamed Tom and Seth for the mysterious disappearance of the other six, but she was only partly correct.

She didn't know about the *one*.

Annie and Kathleen delivered one whole pie, spicy and warm, to my spot outside by the fence.

Kathleen patted my head. "It's a sneak treat. You work hard, too, Judge." She sat the pie at my feet. Annie dumped a bowlful of French vanilla ice cream, *plunk,* on top.

"S'right, Judge. You 'serve the best," Annie said.

As I looked at the ice cream melting into its bed of flaky warmth, I realized that was exactly what I had: the best.

We were really crowded on the four-hour trip to southern Illinois. Maggie had squeezed apples into every possible nook and cranny of the station wagon.

We could see Great-Gramps's farmhouse from the highway. Annie spotted it first.

I had to give Maggie and Grammy credit for planning for a crowd. There were already several cars in the driveway. Even though Grammy's house in town is plenty big, her yard has only a city yard. Great-Gramps has forty acres and a king-sized wraparound porch.

Tom whispered something to Maggie about second cousins twice removed, and they both laughed.

Maggie loves a family party.

Henry came.

It always makes my day.

Henry Von Girard, Grammy's arrogant dachshund, fancies himself the Black Knight of canines. In his presence, anything else that barks is a mere peasant.

I was very grateful for those forty acres. Maybe I could lose myself.

Annie forgot to bring the orange ball that she and Henry always played with, so they used a Red Delicious apple.

Maura didn't know it was a one-on-one game of catch. She pulled herself up on a nearby bushel and tossed apples.

Zap. Ouch, right on my ear.

Maura laughed while I winced.

She threw again.

I ducked.

That kid has an arm!

So Henry and Annie had their game of catch, and Maura and I had our game.

Dodge Apple.

Aunt Phyllis came to my rescue.

She swooped Maura into a warm hug and popped a bonbon into my mouth. "You're the best, big fella. Nary a gripe."

I felt better instantly.

Tables had been set up on the porch, everyone had brought food, and games were being played on a picnic-sized oilcloth on the lawn. Warm sun and the slightest of breezes made the day perfect.

Seth and Kathleen rode the horses. Gramps said that as a favor to the doctor who boarded them, the animals should be exercised.

Some favor. The kids just loved it.

Great-Gramps got out the small tractor with the wood-hauling wagon. He pulled Maura and Annie and Henry in it. The second time around the potato field, he invited me.

Henry wasn't too happy about the extra passenger in *his* chariot, but the girls were giggling, and it was worth it to feel the wind on my ears. Anyway, once I was in, Henry couldn't get out, whether he wanted to share the ride with me or not.

He buried his nose in the corner.

We bounced merrily along for nearly a half-hour. It was great fun until Great-Gramps noticed we were low on gas and decided to stop. I bounded out first, and Great-Gramps took Maura and Annie back up to the house. He came back a few minutes later, parking the tractor in a spot facing the barn.

Henry, still sulking, remained in the wagon, his nose buried under some wood shavings. He paid no attention to the fact the tractor had stopped and we'd left.

When Grammy finally called us for dinner, there was practically a stampede of hungry relatives trying to get to the porch. They left behind their games, their cards, and the oilcloth.

The one family member who didn't come promptly was Henry. When we realized it, we all went to the end of the porch and called him.

Henry saw us waiting for his entrance and decided to give us a show. He puffed out his chest and pranced forward like a Spanish dancer. He took three steps to the end of the wagon and sailed to the ground.

Except there was something different about the wagon's new parking spot.

Oooosh.

Well—what it was—there's a certain ingredient found on farms that cows and horses are responsible for—the smell and texture—well—

Annie skipped down the hill to meet Henry. "Oooooo! Henry, phewy. Cow poopee!"

Now the whole world knew.

Pa got a pail of water and came to help, but Henry wasn't having any.

He ran, and Pa sloshed the water right behind him.

I tried to head Henry off, but he just swished through my legs and kept running.

The oilcloth, the cards, the games were in his path.

Thank goodness everything was washable.

He left little trails of his personal disaster on all he touched.

I almost felt sorry for Henry for the first time in my life when I realized where he was heading —down the road and to the pond. He charged to the old wooden pier way ahead of Pa. Henry turned around with one of those "I'd rather do it myself" faces and then dived.

In midair his ears gave the illusion of a perfect swan dive, but his splash sounded more like a belly flop.

It hardly mattered. By the time Henry paddled to shore, the family was cheering and clapping. He shook himself dry and paraded to the

farmhouse like a grand marshal.

I had to hand it to him.

Henry was the only dog I knew who could fall into a pile of manure and win a hearty applause.

Chapter 5

We ate and ate and ate.

I don't know whether it was the bacon or the yellow mustard that made Grammy's potato salad special, but I could have eaten myself silly. That plus the chicken, the ham, the fresh corn and green beans, and Aunt Phyllis's pasta dish— they were sensational.

People were starting to leave when Great-Gramps excused himself to bring in the cows. Everyone offered to help, but he turned them all down. A few years back, Lula had convinced him to buy a milking machine. In the months after his injury, it had made it possible for him to return to farm work smoothly and quickly. The milking machine was a technological marvel, and Great-Gramps had stopped calling it Lula's new-fangled machine within weeks of its installation. Once the cows stepped into their stalls, nearly everything was automatic.

The hardest part was bringing in the cows.

One stubborn cow could make the whole dozen balk, especially if it was Bossy Lou. She was lead cow, and on some muggy days—Great-Gramps claimed it had something to do with the barometric pressure dropping very rapidly—she would simply lie down, trying the patience even of Great-Gramps. But he always found a way to coax her up to the barn.

Today, the cows had wandered out of sight. Probably we had disrupted their routine. I watched Great-Gramps put on his old fishing hat with its bright red band and colored buttons, and pick up his big red bandanna.

Henry, now smelling like the aftershave that Grammy had generously applied to his fur, had fallen asleep on the porch glider with Annie. Seth and Kathleen had put the horses back in the barn, and Aunt Phyllis was putting away the now spotless Tripoli game. The rest of the relatives were loading apples into their cars. Maggie had given everyone an apple pie and a full bushel.

There were two bushels and three pies left for Great-Gramps.

"Maybe we should come down next weekend with another load," Maggie said.

Aunt Phyllis groaned. "Please don't. I will burst from more party food."

"I have a better idea," Pa offered. "Those apples can be stored for a long time in a cool corner of your garage, Maggie. We'll just come visit every weekend and cook and preserve in your kitchen. . . ."

Maggie held up her hands, palms out, to ward off any more bright ideas like that. "No, thanks, friends."

"Great-Gramps is a little slow today getting back," Tom said, looking down toward the barn.

"The cows were clear at the other end of the pasture, Dad," Kathleen said.

"It's a good walk," Seth agreed.

"Sure," Tom answered. But I noticed he kept an eye on the barn.

Was it taking too long?

I'd never really paid much attention before, but since Tom seemed concerned and no one needed my help at the house, I thought I'd wander down and see for myself. Grammy and Maggie had put all the food away anyway.

It was the second prettiest time of day.

I've always been partial to sunrises, but this sunset was a beauty. Wild lilies that hadn't given in to the cold of the brisk fall nights still lined the fencing. Neat rows of corn furrows were outlined against the orange glow of sunset.

I couldn't see Great-Gramps, so I trotted a little faster. The soft ground slid a bit underneath me.

Had Great-Gramps changed into his work boots? I hadn't noticed. Some of the muddy spots were a bit slippery.

Well, he knew his way around better than me. Didn't he?

A funny gnawing began in my stomach.

I reached the cows. They were huddled in the farthest corner, just as Kathleen had said.

I stood very still and listened.

I had no idea where to look. Would he have stopped somewhere to rest? Could he have changed his mind and gone back for help?

No, I would have met him. He'd taken the main path, the same one I had just covered. Where was he?

I barked loudly. If he would just answer. . . . But only Bossy Lou mooed back.

My heart was beginning to pound, and I wondered if I should run for help. But time might be important. If he'd fallen or become suddenly ill . . .

I barked again.

Silence.

Bossy Lou went back to her grazing.

I waited, then barked once more.

I heard a hoarse, husky voice. Just barely. "Judge."

Where was he?

I made a complete circle, slowly, and listened again.

"Judge . . . here."

It seemed to be coming from behind and below me.

I walked a few feet back toward the house.

"Good boy." The voice seemed stronger. I must be getting warm.

"Down. Down . . ."

The old bridge was nearly hidden by wild mulberry bushes. No one ever used it. It was on the other side of the pasture fence. Much of the bridge's wood was rotten, and the bank was steep and jagged down to the creek.

Why on earth would Great-Gramps have gone down there?

I found him at the water's edge. There was

blood on his head and on his good hand, and he looked very white. A craggy rock had stopped his fall, but he was holding his chest where it must have caught his side.

I pushed my way down the bank and gently licked the wound on his hand. "Not to worry, Judge. It's the . . . the cheap hand. The one I grew . . . myself." He was speaking very slowly, but he managed a smile.

His eyes blinked slowly. "Judge . . . the . . . the . . . hat . . ."

Then he closed them again, and his head fell softly to the side.

Gramps?

I knew what I had to do. And it had nothing to do with picking up that dumb hat.

I raced for help, faster than I'd ever run in my life.

Great-Gramps had to be all right!

I didn't make it to the house.

Tom had already started toward me. He'd still been watching from the porch, and as soon as I came up the hill, he headed my way. He saw my face. "Judge, where?"

He knew.

Suddenly there were lots of footsteps behind us.

In no time we were all scrambling down the gully.

Tom got to Great-Gramps first and began shouting orders.

"Get Doc Higgins on the phone, Aunt Phyllis. Pa, bring the car down as close as you can. Kathleen, get some blankets, hurry now! Seth, someone has to stay with Annie and Maura, go on!"

"He's going to be fine. It always looks worse than it is." Maggie was squeezing my fur as she tried to be reassuring.

An awful acid taste kept me from swallowing.

The running stopped.

The praying started.

Please, Great-Gramps, please. Be all right.

Chapter 6

Doc Higgins could have been two hundred years old. Or he could have been fifty. He had that kind of semilined face, white hair, and remarkably trim, energetic body. Doc had been at Great-Gramps's wedding, had delivered all of Lula's children, and had doctored the farm animals before a veterinarian had established a local practice. He still held office hours three days a week and filled in for the vet on vacation days. Doc lived two miles up the road, and he arrived so fast, he must have flown.

"I can't tell you too much, Tom," he told us after spending nearly two hours with Great-Gramps. "I've taped the ribs. He's got two that are going to be real painful on that right side, and I've stitched his hand and his forehead. He's going to be awful sore, but . . ."

Doc Higgins accepted a cup of coffee from Maggie and sipped slowly. There was a long pause, but nobody interrupted. Even Annie and Maura were perfectly still.

". . . but I suspect he'll be okay if he wants to," he finished finally.

Everyone in the room sighed with relief. Even Henry.

"The head injury?" Grammy asked.

"Not so bad. It bled, and that's good. Mild concussion, maybe. We could take him in for X rays to put your mind at ease, but I think the move would do him more harm," Doc answered.

"Well, if you're sure he shouldn't be hospitalized." Maggie was nearly whispering.

"Maggie, I'm not concerned that I'll be slapped with a malpractice suit for not making enough tests. Clarence is my friend. I think the best thing would be for someone to take care of him right here. Keeping his spirits up is as important as anything else. We need to keep the pain down—but then Clarence is no stranger to pain."

Maggie refilled the doc's cup.

"Well, I can stay," Grammy said.

"The cows, Mom." It was Maggie. She looked very serious. "Tom took care of them tonight but . . ."

"What?" Grammy didn't understand.

But I did. Milk cows don't take vacations.

"She's right." Pa stood up. "You may be the greatest at nursing old men"—he winked at Grammy—"but you are no farm wife. And I can't leave the drugstore twice a day to handle it. Those are peak hours."

Tom was thoughtful. "I can take a few days off work."

"It's going to take more than a few days," Maggie said.

Doc Higgins said nothing. The kids said nothing.

I wanted to say something.

Two weeks? Three? If the healing was smooth, maybe, but if pneumonia or some complication set in, it was up for grabs how long Great-Gramps would need help.

"Well, as I see it, we have two choices," Tom said matter-of-factly. "Sell the cows or hire someone."

"And how do you think Great-Gramps would feel about that?" Maggie walked over to Maura and picked her up. Maura had not been fussing —it was Maggie who needed Maura's hug. She usually did this before making some major decision.

"I'll do it," she said simply.

I looked at my big klutzy paws. I wished I could do it.

Henry was clicking his teeth.

"I'll stay here and manage the cows. You can miss a few days of work to show me what to do, Tom. The kids and I will handle it." Her hand swept the room. "You can come down weekends until Great-Gramps is strong enough to run things himself.

"Take us out of school?" Seth asked.

"You can make it up. You're good-enough students," Maggie said. She stopped pacing with Maura and sat on the couch by Kathleen. "You kids can't stay with Dad, he's gone too much. I can make arrangements with Sister Mary Clare to have your homework mailed."

"My teaching certificate's still valid," Aunt Phyllis added. "Maybe I can give you tests and act as an official tutor."

Kathleen was chewing her lip. I wondered if she was thinking of those spelling bees she'd miss. "You're right, Mom. I think there are a few things we can learn here anyway."

"Lula managed it by herself for nearly four months while Great-Gramps was in therapy, and she was sixty years old," Maggie said.

"Spring chicken!" Aunt Phyllis declared.

"Who knows, maybe I'll even lose ten pounds!" Maggie was pinching her midriff.

I held my stomach in. Talk of diets always improved my posture.

"In that case, why don't you do my job at the construction site and I'll stay here?" Tom was smiling, too.

Pa was lighting his pipe. "What I want to know is, who is going to break the terrific news to Great-Gramps that the O'Rileys are taking over his farm!"

It was a wonder the laughter didn't wake Great-Gramps right then.

By the time the kids went to bed, a lot of the anticipated problems had been ironed out.

Since Great-Gramps didn't have a washer and dryer, Aunt Phyllis offered to "pick up and deliver" twice a week. Pa and Grammy went into town for extra bedding and dishes, and Tom went along to pick up some groceries to feed the extra hungry mouths for a few days.

When they got back and Maggie unpacked a

box of extra clothes that Grammy had sent along, she found some gentle face soap at the bottom. Grammy was thoughtful like that.

We were going to miss home and Decatur and some of the little luxuries we might have taken for granted.

I couldn't help thinking of the pool and the hot Indian summer days that would hit southern Illinois soon. I knew I wasn't the only one who would miss home.

But this was an adventure of love.

One by one, all the family tiptoed into the downstairs front bedroom and kissed a sleeping Great-Gramps good night.

Kathleen and Seth made the upstairs beds with Grammy's linens for the four children. Tom and Maggie took the back bedroom downstairs. I had a large straw rug on the front porch.

It was quiet, finally.

Chapter 7

I was too fidgety to sleep.

I felt sort of responsible for all of Great-Gramps's acreage, so I began a long walk from farm building to chicken house, around the old silo, and past the woodpile and milk house.

The air had the crinkle of a fall night, and stars were everywhere. There was so little industry in this part of the state that pollution didn't obscure their brightness. I loved it here. It wasn't home, but it was special.

The horses were quiet. The cows looked like statues on their side of the main barn. I thought it best not to look in the chicken house.

Even city dogs know some things instinctively.

Everything seemed to be in order.

I walked all the way to the end of the pasture near the spot where I'd found Great-Gramps. I still didn't understand what he'd been doing there. Few cars used the highway near the fence, but when a huge truck rumbled along, the old bridge rattled like an echo.

It just wasn't like Great-Gramps to take chances. No one used that rickety bridge, yet by the light of the sky, I could see the busted place where Great-Gramps had fallen through.

That's when I thought of the hat.

It seemed funny that it had been the only thing he'd mentioned. The hat. He hadn't even said *"my* hat."

I guess he needed it for calling the cows.

Carefully, I scooted down the bank again:

It gave me an odd feeling, seeing the spot where Great-Gramps had fallen, but if the hat was important to him, maybe I should bring it back to the farmhouse.

I spotted it, caught on a piece of driftwood. It was hanging next to a faded burlap bag.

That was odd. Someone must have tossed it there from the highway. Great Gramps wouldn't have littered.

I started toward the hat.

That's when I saw it move.

Wind?

No, the air was still.

I held my breath and looked again. I'm not exactly crazy about night creatures, but I had to reach the hat.

Something moved again.

It wasn't the hat. It was the burlap bag.

Please don't be a snake, I thought.

Please don't be a rat either. I hate those things.

I grabbed the hat in my mouth and prepared to run.

That's when I heard the slightest whimper.

I knew.

Two small black eyes and a black nose were watching me.

This was no wild creature.

It was a puppy, a frightened pitiful pup, probably thrown from the road by . . . I didn't dare think of what fate had been meant for this little character. It was shivering, and its curly ears were matted and dirty. When I moved closer, it disappeared back inside the burlap bag.

The drawstring around the top of the bag had come loose when it caught on the driftwood. The bag was hanging just inches above the creek, high enough to keep the pup from drowning. The pup was either too weak or too scared to venture from the bag.

Great-Gramps must have seen it. And when he went to investigate. . . .

No matter how tired everyone was, this was a rescue that wouldn't wait until morning.

I ran back to the house, Great-Gramps's hat still in my mouth.

Poor Seth was the only family member besides Maura who didn't sleep with his head under a pillow. I didn't want to wake Great-Gramps by barking, so my next best wake-up call was a St. Bernard kiss.

The effect was as jarring as a California earthquake.

"Judge, what? It's the middle of the night," he begged.

But I didn't quit. When he finally sat up, I handed him his slippers.

We proceeded to Maggie and Tom's room on the double.

"Mom, Dad," Seth whispered excitedly. "Something's wrong. Judge got me up."

It was a loud whisper, but Tom was in a deep sleep.

Maggie looked at me, not fully understanding.

I grabbed her arm in my mouth and pulled gently.

Maggie rubbed her head and pushed her hair

back from her eyes. She was just barely awake.

I kept tugging.

"What is it, Judge? Maura? Great-Gramps?"

Maggie was sitting up now.

"No, I checked on them as we went by," Seth said softly. "The Judge keeps pointing to the door. I think it's something outside."

Maggie shook Tom's shoulder. "Tom. Tom."

Tom made a strange swallowing sound and mumbled, "It's just the house settling."

"Tom, please." Maggie tried again.

"Sounds . . . louder . . . in the . . . country." He went back to sleep.

Maggie started to try again but changed her mind. "Okay, Judge. Let's see what this is all about."

She got out of bed. When she realized she had no slippers, she looked for her shoes, but she couldn't find them in the dark. She grabbed Tom's wool work shirt, threw it over her night-gown, and off we went.

Kathleen had been disturbed by the commotion and came down in time to meet us at the door. "Whatever it is, Mom, I'm going, too."

Kathleen grabbed a poncho from a hook by the door and followed.

Maggie looked down at her bare feet and the

soft ground oozing between her toes and hesitated. She probably remembered Henry's surprise landing.

Kathleen spotted the tractor and pointed. "Seth?"

"Sure," he answered. Great-Gramps had let him drive the tractor on our last visit. Seth started the tractor, pulled up to where we were waiting, saluted, and said, "Taxi, ladies?"

Maggie jumped up front, and Kathleen got in the wagon.

I ran ahead as wagon master.

"This had better be good, big fella," Maggie was shouting over the sputtering motor, "or you won't taste whipped cream till the twenty-first century."

Maggie fumbled in the toolbox and found a flashlight as we bobbed down the path. Seth stopped the tractor at the top of the hill, and I led them on foot to the spot by the water. Seth had trouble finding the parking brake, and when he finally followed, he slid down the bank and into the creek in his haste to catch up. His feet and seat were soaked.

Maggie tore her nightgown on a rock.

But Kathleen, who was the first to spot the reason for the emergency, lifted the scared little puppy, burlap bag and all, and held it close.

"Mom, oh, Mom," was all she could say.

The pup stopped shivering in Kathleen's arms. Kathleen wrapped her bathrobe carefully around what looked like a springer spaniel, black and white and painfully frail.

In spite of the mud and wet, the marks of a well-bred dog were evident. It made me sick to think that such a pup could be mistreated.

Kathleen was petting the tiny dog and whispering to it in a soothing, motherly way. Once the shivering stopped, the pup was very, very still.

Chapter 8

When Maggie's third attempt to reach the town veterinarian was met with an answering service —he was on an emergency—she called the only other knight in shining armor she could think of.

Doc Higgins.

He wasn't wearing his armor.

When he arrived and took off his trench coat, no one needed to ask the dumb question, "Did we get you out of bed?" He had on a pair of red jogging pants, a blue paisley pajama top, and sneakers with no socks.

Tom had gotten up after all. He was waiting for us when the tractor sputtered on its last trickle of gas and we had run the final few yards

up the hill. He'd sensed something was wrong when Maggie was no longer asleep beside him. Then Maura had started to fuss, something she never does in the middle of the night. But this hadn't been an ordinary night, and the Portacrib wasn't the same as her own bed. We all gathered around the wood stove while Doc Higgins examined the newest patient.

"So this is what Clarence was after down by the creek," Doc Higgins finally said. "I hope it wasn't in vain."

We all knew what he meant. No one spoke.

Kathleen handed the doctor a towel that had been warming on top of the wood stove. He wrapped up the little pup. Then Kathleen took the pup in her arms and sat at the edge of the couch, as close as she dared to the fire.

"I just don't understand the meanness of it," Doc Higgins went on. "The mother's milk runs out, and they . . ."

He didn't have to finish. We knew. Someone, somewhere, had just not wanted the puppy.

"She's got pneumonia, for sure," Doc said then, "and we have to worry about distemper. Some of the little ones never recover from that."

Seth picked up Maura and handed her a pacifier. She didn't need it, but I guess it gave him something to do.

"She's going to make it," Maggie said firmly. "Any little thing that can get me up in the middle of the night—well, it won't be for nothing."

"She's wanted now," Kathleen put in. "If she feels that, I think it will help." Her voice cracked as she spoke.

Tom shook his head. I knew he didn't want to get their hopes up.

"She'll need a name," Seth said. "Something that goes with O'Riley."

A noisy discussion got in gear. It must have been getting quite loud, and very intense, because I was the only one who noticed a wobbly figure in the doorway.

"*So!* You found my Margaret!" It was Great-Gramps, and his smile was the happiest thing we had seen all day. A little figure dragging a Strawberry Shortcake sleeping bag ambled up, tugged at his knee, and said, "Margrit? Margrit who? Is dere more company?"

Even a three-year-old's tug was too much for Great-Gramps. He slid to the arm of the couch just as his knees began to buckle.

"Gramps!" Maggie was at his side instantly, fluffing the pillow behind him, scooting Kathleen and the pup aside to give him room.

It was a case of too many people moving too fast. Doc Higgins grabbed his black bag on the

floor beside him and headed for Great-Gramps.
Tom was already on his way across the room, his
size-twelve foot landing on Strawberry Shortcake's smiling face. Annie picked that moment
to yank her sleeping bag onto the couch.

Hup . . . two . . . hoist . . .

Bingo.

Tom's flailing arms volleyed Doc Higgins's
black bag toward the ceiling. Tom didn't duck,
and it collided with his eye on its way down.

Great-Gramps was holding his side trying to
stifle a chuckle. "Tell you what, why don't you all
take two aspirin and call me in the morning?" he
said.

"Please," Maggie cried, "no more emergen-
cies!"

Kathleen was standing in front of the stove
still holding the pup. "Why did you call her Margaret?"

Seth was curious, too. "Is this somebody's pup
that we have to give back?"

Doc Higgins interrupted before Great-
Gramps could answer. "If we're going to give
anybody back, it should be Clarence—to a ken-
nel!" he said. "Didn't anyone ever explain to you
about rest and recuperation?" he asked Great-
Gramps.

"Yup. Man by the name of Higgins. How is my Margaret?" Great-Gramps asked. "She looked a little the worse for wear when I found her today."

Seth and Kathleen both sighed with relief. They knew with the sound of the word "found" that the pup could stay.

"She's not in terrific shape, Clarence, but if she has any of the family's stubbornness, she might make it." Doc Higgins put his stethoscope away and closed his black bag. "Would you consider setting a good example, my friend?"

"We can't have any sickies on my farm. Getting well is the only practical thing to do," said Great-Gramps, pushing himself to the end of the couch nearer the stove, where Kathleen was standing. Raising his good hand, he gently cuffed the ears of the sleeping pup. "Okay, Miss Margaret. Your first job as a member of this family is to get well."

It was as if she had been called for the first time. Miss Margaret opened her eyes and, ever so slightly, lifted her head.

Then, once more, she fell softly to sleep.

Before Doc Higgins left, Tom gave him the information for a dog license application. The doc's office was right by the county building, and he'd offered to pick up some dog tags first thing in the morning.

We made only one concession on the name. Instead of "Miss" Margaret O'Riley, it became *Ms.* Margarette O'Riley. The fancy spelling was Seth's idea, and the Ms.—well, with four O'Riley ladies, does it need explaining? When Tom and Seth got on either side of Great-Gramps to help him back to bed, I heard him mumble something about the "next" generation—but they were all smiling.

Ms. Margarette O'Riley. She was ours.

Chapter 9

Great-Gramps wouldn't tell us why he called the pup Margarette. It became something of a game for everyone to make regular guesses. Tom teased that it was the name of one of Great-Gramps's old girlfriends. Maggie thought it was a namesake for her. Kathleen claimed it had to be after the famous queen of Denmark.

When Kathleen said that, Ms. Margarette's left eye opened and closed in a very slow wink.

Great-Gramps just smiled and kept silent.

I looked at the sweet black face with the sad eyes and curly ears and figured it didn't matter where the name came from. The fact was, it surely fit.

Those jokes about the name couldn't hide our real feelings about Ms. Margarette, though. We were all worried.

The first two days were the hardest.

We couldn't get her to eat.

Ms. Margarette was so tiny that even Doc Higgins wouldn't guess her age. He said when she lost her baby teeth, we'd know she was three months old, but until then, it was anyone's guess.

If she made it to three months, he added.

Kathleen hardly let the pup out of her sight.

She tried feeding her with a baby bottle first, but Ms. Margarette refused it. Maggie made baby formula instead of milk, but that didn't change things either. Tom tried giving her tea and honey through a medicine dropper. She took some, but not nearly enough. Seth put warm, soft oatmeal in the palm of his hand, but even that brought limited success. Annie alternately praised and scolded her, hoping for a reaction.

There wasn't any.

I stayed with her and ate all my meals where she could see me. I thought setting a good example might do it.

Great-Gramps set his own good example, too, just as Doc Higgins had requested that first night. He ate everything Maggie set in front of him, he went to bed early at night, and he took good, long naps. He started taking regular walks, short at first, but longer each day. It may have been painful, but he never let on. At the end of the first full week, the bottle of pain pills Doc Higgins had left for him to take "as needed" was still full.

Doc Higgins kept dropping by. He always said he was out jogging, but on the afternoon when he arrived wearing penny loafers, we knew he was just being kind. He spent at least half his visit scolding Great-Gramps for getting up and about too soon, but he kept winking at Tom and Maggie. Great-Gramps was going to be fine.

But Ms. Margarette—well, Doc just kept shaking his head. "She's got to eat," he told us. "We've got to build her up." He left vitamin powder to stir into her milk, and suggested we take her in the warm sun outside.

There was nothing else he could recommend.

Maggie and Tom had their hands full mastering the farm. Tom spent a lot of time on the phone directing his business long-distance, and Maggie handled cows, chickens, and horses as best she could.

Seth learned to wield an ax like a veteran. He

worked at building up the woodpile into a respectable winter supply. Great-Gramps shouldn't have to worry about reinjuring his cracked ribs with that job.

Kathleen did a little of everything. She went to the person who needed help the most and pitched in.

We were into the second week when Kathleen put Maura and Annie down for an early nap and she and Great-Gramps took Ms. Margarette outside. Great-Gramps was grateful to have company in the sunshine. Kathleen lay a blanket down for the pup, just past the porch.

Kathleen set Ms. Margarette down and went to get a lawn chair for Great-Gramps.

Great-Gramps leaned on me for support while he waited.

Ms. Margarette was watching the leaves. It wasn't windy, but there was enough air to move the leaves in a slow dance on the lawn near her blanket. Ms. Margarette's ears picked up the crackling sound and her eyes were very wide. A singing cardinal flew overhead, and the puppy cocked her head. When Kathleen came back out with the chair, Ms. Margarette lifted her ears in the direction of the crunching noise under Kathleen's feet. The sound held her attention for a bit, then she turned back to the other leaves dancing nearest her.

Great-Gramps sat down, still watching the puppy. "Kathleen, we've been misreading our patient," he said.

I didn't know exactly what he meant, but I parked myself by the blanket to watch.

Kathleen started to bend down to pick up the little spaniel.

"No, Kathleen. I think Ms. Margarette would like to find her own way." Great-Gramps caught Kathleen's hand. "The sounds, Kathleen—let's let her play detective. We've forgotten that spaniels are sporting by nature."

He motioned Kathleen to help him back onto the porch and then sent her into the kitchen for a bowl of Rice Krispies and milk.

Rice Krispies?

When Kathleen returned, she placed the bowl on the ground some four feet from the blanket. Then she went back to the porch to sit with Great-Gramps.

Rice Krispies?

Then I heard the snap, crackle, and pop. So did Ms. Margarette. The Rice Krispies were making louder music than the leaves.

Ms. Margarette's head came up. She listened.

She raised herself up on her front paws.

Kathleen went back into the house for three more bowls and put them around the lawn.

Ms. Margarette stood up.

She was swaying, but she stayed up.

We knew she would investigate the sounds.

Eventually she noticed all of the dishes. When she stuck her nose in the first bowl, then licked her mouth, she seemed incredibly pleased with herself. She was too tiny to consume all the cereal after those days of near-starvation, but she did taste some of what was in each bowl.

That was a beginning.

Ms. Margarette was going to be just fine, too.

Chapter 10

I'm not sure whom I learned the most from in the weeks that followed. It didn't take long for me to figure out that both farming and family required team effort. The more everyone pitched in, the smoother things went. Leisure time was infrequent. If there'd been a pool at the farm, we couldn't have used it. Those wonderful lazy summer days in Decatur were just a pleasant memory. Maggie lost four pounds the first week and would have lost more except that on laundry and tutoring days, Aunt Phyllis brought a care package from Grammy that replenished our sweets supply.

In a little more than a week's time, Ms. Margarette's weight doubled and her energy level put us all to shame. Kathleen was forever running after her. Ms. Margarette wanted to see the world, the sooner the better. At least once a day she'd slip away, and the whole family would have to join in and search for her. She chased the mice in the barn, fell into the horses' oat pail, and swam in the water trough. One day, when we were sure we had lost her—it took Kathleen over an hour to find her—she had found an old tennis ball, carried it to the chicken house, and roosted on it. The hens never even squawked. Ms. Margarette could have been one of them.

If I came within fifty feet of their eggs, they carried on for hours.

They didn't trust me. I had broken my own rule about avoiding the farm fowl on one of our Ms. Margarette hunts. I'd slipped into the chicken coop, and a battalion of pecking feathers had attacked me. I managed to upset four perches before I escaped.

It hadn't been the time of day for scrambled eggs.

Great-Gramps set up a bell system after that. *His* bell system. He found some small Christmas jingles and put three on Ms. Margarette's collar and ten on mine. Ms. Margarette was so fond of investigating noises that she took to following me around. When my louder jingle stopped, hers did, too, as she stopped to listen.

Ms. Margarette's ringy-dingy got to me at first, but after a while it was like having a whistling shadow, and I kind of liked it.

Ms. Margarette still did her share of exploring, but more and more, we did it together.

She was so at home on the farm with all the animals. When Maggie brought the cows up to the milk house, Ms. Margarette and Great-Gramps would sit and watch each one come in, as if they were counting children.

Once, when Bossy Lou changed her mind and backed off instead of going right in the barn, Ms. Margarette left Great-Gramps's side and stood directly behind her.

I was sure she'd be trampled. Instead, Bossy Lou changed directions.

Ms. Margarette had a handle on cow telepathy. Eventually, we all began to notice her gift.

When Tom took off for a second trip to Waterloo, Iowa, Great-Gramps was walking as far as the barn a couple of times a day. Maggie had begun to get the hang of her farm routine, too. So when Seth and Kathleen finished their homework that second week, Maggie invited everyone down to the pasture to watch her bring in the cows.

Seth brought Great-Gramps and Annie and Maura on the tractor. Kathleen and Ms. Margarette and I trotted behind them.

I was the only one who arrived slightly out of breath.

"Okay, kids," said Maggie, climbing under the fence with Great-Gramps's fishing hat and red bandanna. "Watch this." She marched over to the end of the fence and started waving the hat and making a strange popping sound with her mouth.

Annie called it letting the air out of a kiss.

Only nothing happened.

The cows didn't move.

Maggie tried again, a bit more determinedly.

This time a couple of them moved. Bossy Lou and one other mooing cow lay down.

I could see Maggie was embarrassed.

"I don't understand it," she said mostly to herself.

She tried again, waving the bandanna right at Bossy Lou's eye level. "Bossy Lou!" she yelled.

I knew that wouldn't help. One thing cows don't do is answer to a name.

The reason we called the lead cow Bossy Lou

was because it was the name on her cowbell. She only got the bell in the first place because she was standing closest to the fence the day Lula brought it back from a farm auction in Pope County.

Bossy Lou's rise to power came with the clang.

Maggie waved the hat again.

The popping noises got more desperate.

Great-Gramps was fidgeting. If he helped, it would make Maggie seem foolish. And if he didn't help . . .

Ms. Margarette moved in for a better look. She folded her skinny front legs over the bottom rung of the fence and stared.

I squeezed through a gap in the gate.

Then I went behind the cows and growled.

A bad move. Two more cows lay down.

Frustration wrinkled Maggie's forehead. It had been a piece of cake all the days without an audience.

Maybe if someone put the bell around my neck, I could pass for Bossy Lou.

But I didn't have to.

Ms. Margarette crawled under the fence and walked right up to Bossy Lou. The little spaniel jumped, her nose clanging Bossy Lou's bell.

And Bossy Lou was off to the races, quickly followed by her lazy partners.

Ms. Margarette, hopping and skipping between them, rode herd all the way back to the barn.

"Well, I'll be," Great-Gramps said softly.

Everyone was terribly proud.

Maggie tied the red bandanna under Ms. Margarette's chin, and Seth and Kathleen and Annie applauded. Maura tried to clap her hands, too, but since one hand was needed for balance, she landed unceremoniously on her rump.

I got one paw under her in time to soften the blow.

Ms. Margarette stayed with Maggie and the cows all through milking time. Kathleen had to call her three times for supper.

That was dedication.

When it was finally time for bed and Kathleen led the puppy into the big room with the stove where the spaniel had been sleeping, Ms. Margarette whined.

We hadn't heard that sound since the first night. During all her discomfort, Ms. Margarette had been stoic and quiet, but now she began a low-grade howl.

"Ms. Margarette!" Kathleen scolded.

"I reckon she's trying to tell us something," Great-Gramps said.

He opened the door, and the pup went charging back to the barn.

She found a spot where the wood had weathered and splintered, leaving a small gap under the big barn door. First she peaked in underneath, then she arranged some stray leaves and backed her back half into the opening.

We watched from the doorway as she snuggled in.

"Won't she be cold?" Kathleen asked.

"Nope," Great-Gramps answered. "If she takes to sleeping out, her fur will thicken naturally. She'll be even prettier, too."

"But she's so little," Kathleen protested.

"There's not much to size. If there was, a cow could catch a rabbit." Great-Gramps answered slowly, giving Kathleen time to think. No one else spoke.

"She might run off. . . ." Kathleen was still not convinced.

"Might. Might not." Great-Gramps let her think about that, too. "But she's got a lot of good reasons to stay."

I was still trying to picture a cow chasing a rabbit.

Kathleen started to argue more but stopped herself. She and Great-Gramps watched Ms.

Margarette fall peacefully to sleep.

"Well, I suppose it won't hurt just this once," she said finally.

Just this once?

I wondered about that.

Chapter 11

There was one Rolls Royce in Metropolis, Illinois, and Aunt Phyllis drove it.

No, actually, she commandeered it. The only thing missing was her captain's hat. The car was fourteen years old, but just as bright and shiny as the day it rolled off the showroom floor in St. Louis. Aunt Phyllis and Uncle George had made the Missouri trip to protest a bad set of tires on another car. When they received no satisfaction from the dealer, they elected to trade "up."

Boy did they trade *up!*

The first laundry day, Aunt Phyllis drove up Great-Gramps's driveway at a very respectable three and one-half miles per hour so the country dust wouldn't muss the spit shine on the car's chrome. The second time, she sped at the wicked rate of fifteen miles an hour and handed Seth a dusting chamois when she got out of the car. The third visit, she tore in at her time-is-money thirty-nine miles an hour, dashed to the phone, and made a four o'clock appointment at the local car wash.

Aunt Phyllis was nothing less than superefficient.

It seemed inconsistent to see such an ample woman step out of an elegant limousine carrying two baskets of laundry, but that's exactly what she did, every Tuesday and Thursday. She tromped into the house before the dust settled in the wake behind her, and within minutes of passing out the clean clothes, she began her teaching duties.

When I saw her coming, I made it a point to run ahead and push open the door for her. It wasn't just to be polite. If I stayed outside, the dust stirred up by Aunt Phyllis and her car would give me a coughing fit.

Superefficiency, one discovers, is not without drawbacks.

"She's coming," Kathleen announced one sunny Tuesday morning.

Maggie set down her cup of tea—her first, though she had been up since five—and went to the kitchen to pour coffee for Aunt Phyllis. "Mass must have run a little long this morning. It's nearly nine, and she's always been here by eight forty-five."

I met Aunt Phyllis out front. She put a large shopping bag that smelled of pine and ammonia around my neck. Seth met us at the kitchen door. Aunt Phyllis exchanged her two baskets for the open arms of Annie and Maura. She slipped the bag off my neck and onto the counter and began passing out hugs. "You behaving yourself, Great-Gramps?"

She didn't give him a chance to answer. She kept talking. "Got a surprise for you, Maggie. I made an appointment for you to get a haircut and a facial in thirty minutes. And after that, go see your mother. She's treating you to lunch." Aunt Phyllis tossed Maggie the keys to the Rolls. "Won't take no for an answer."

Who could answer?

"It's my Mother's Day treat," she said.

Aunt Phyllis started passing out the graded homework. "Seth, I'm not at all impressed with this book report. . . ."

Maggie looked at the keys, grinned at the kids,

saw Great-Gramps's nodding smile, and went for her purse.

No one seemed to mind that Mother's Day had occurred five months before.

"I'll be back in plenty of time to milk," Maggie said when she came back downstairs, "but about the eggs—and there's applesauce cooking . . ." She looked at Kathleen but Seth broke in.

"I'll handle it, Mom," he said.

"Oh, no, you won't, young man," Aunt Phyllis said. "Not until you rewrite this report. I might give you an A for content, but your penmanship is abominable. I can't send this to Sister Mary Clare and still sleep nights."

Great-Gramps stood up. "Annie and I will collect the eggs, and we'll take turns stirring the applesauce."

"Go on, Mom. I'll put Maura in the playpen with her blocks," Kathleen said.

Ms. Margarette squeezed through the playpen posts to be close to the baby, but when Maura began pulling her tail, Ms. Margarette came out the same way she'd gone in.

Kathleen headed for the kitchen to check the applesauce, but Aunt Phyllis stopped her. "Not so fast, Kathleen. This math paper isn't up to your usual standards." She sat Kathleen down, handed her the paper, went to the kitchen herself, stirred the applesauce, and came back before anyone could take a deep breath.

Whew.

"Don't worry about a thing, Maggie. Everything's under control," Aunt Phyllis said.

Control? Why did that word sound so threatening?

What the heck, I wasn't getting any homework graded.

I followed Maggie out to the car to say goodbye.

Ms. Margarette jingled behind me.

"I don't know, Judge," Maggie said as much to herself as to me. "Aunt Phyllis was rather intense this morning, didn't you think? She's never tried to spirit me away before. And that shopping bag . . ."

I thought of those funny smells.

A master plan?

Maggie patted my head and rubbed Ms. Margarette's ears. Once in the car, she spent several minutes studying the dash panel before she took off. She came dangerously close to the end fence post as she turned that monster onto the highway, but she made it.

If she could manage cows, I guess she could learn to maneuver a Rolls.

Great-Gramps and Annie came out with empty baskets and headed for the chicken house. Ms. Margarette and I tagged along.

But I kept my vigil *outside* the shed.

Annie was trying to teach Great-Gramps to sing "A Tisket a Tasket," and he was being a patient student. Ms. Margarette added her tiny bark, but that started the hens squawking, so Great-Gramps postponed the serenade till the job was done.

I joined them at the old pump where Great-Gramps always washed the eggs. It wasn't the greatest job in the world, but Annie and Great-Gramps had a grand time working together.

Great-Gramps spread newspapers on the ground and hooked the wire basket under the pump. Slowly, patiently, he washed each egg. He made a game of passing each one from his "magic" hand to Annie. Once the pump was primed, he let Annie ride up and down on the arm, her feet dangling as it rose. She loved it, and it gave his sore ribs a rest. Annie got cartons from the garage and counted five and a half dozen eggs before they were through.

Ms. Margarette sat close enough to the spigot

to get a dribble of water now and then. Her head shook with delight, making her jingle bells ring. That just made it more fun.

What a puppy.

I headed back to the house while they finished up.

Twenty yards away from the kitchen door, I could smell Aunt Phyllis's cleaning solutions in action. Kathleen and Seth were slaving away at the big dining room table on some homework, while Aunt Phyllis was scrubbing and whistling in the kitchen a mile a minute.

She had exchanged her Italian knit suit for a pair of Great-Gramps's old overalls and one of his plaid shirts. It clashed more than a little with her cameo earrings. She was down on her knees scouring and brushing the linoleum floor. Every now and then, she took off a rubber glove, stood up, and gave the applesauce a stir. It got trickier as she worked herself farther from the stove, but her long arms got the job done.

Ah, Maggie. Your ship is getting shaped.

Kathleen came in once to question a math problem.

"Get my bifocals, hon," Aunt Phyllis directed.

Kathleen slid them onto Aunt Phyllis's nose and held the paper at arm's length in front of her. Without missing a scrubadub, Aunt Phyllis explained the equation.

It was such a nice gesture—Aunt Phyllis understanding Maggie's work load and taking it upon herself to give Maggie the kind of break she needed. I sat on the back step where I could keep track of the kitchen cleaning, the students, and the egg venture. Contentment was raising its peaceful head when . . .

Aunt Phyllis found a flea.

"*AAAAAAAIIIIIIIIIIEEEEEEEEE!* Mercy! Mercy!"

The cows looked up. The chickens screamed. The horses whinnied. Ms. Margarette started her little howl. I barked in sheer surprise. But such sounds were pin drops compared to Aunt Phyllis's indignation.

Seth and Kathleen scrambled into the kitchen, and Annie came scampering up, too.

All because of one little flea. It probably rode in on an egg or something.

It kept hopping all over the linoleum floor, and it took seven minutes before the identification could be absolutely confirmed. At last Great-Gramps (who in his weakened condition had all but run to see what was wrong) caught the little troublemaker between two fingers.

"Is it? *Is it?* It is, isn't it?" Aunt Phyllis was clearly flustered. If it had been a major mudslide, it could not have been more of a challenge to the Clean Queen.

"Yup. 'Fraid so. But there's no cause for alarm." Great-Gramps tried hard to reassure her.

"Cin I see, Great-Gramps?" Annie was pulling at his fingers containing the indestructible critter.

Once more the flea went hopping.

"Oh, thas no s'prise. I saw 'em before—on Judge's rug 'n' by the gurtains. . . ." Annie was bragging, but Aunt Phyllis was horrified.

Seth groaned. Kathleen sighed. Aunt Phyllis took a deep breath.

Annie kept talking. "Boy, they jump real high. Really, really high!"

"Season's almost over," Great-Gramps said. "We'll spray." He caught the flea a second time, flushing it down the drain of the kitchen sink with scalding water.

Aunt Phyllis's eyes were burning a hole in the screen door. She was staring at me.

Hey, wait. I hadn't even scratched. She wouldn't think I'd let a varmint hitch a ride on me. . . .

She turned her scowl toward Ms. Margarette and took a *very* deep breath.

Suddenly, I knew. Pine and ammonia were not the tools of a woman who would settle for mere bug spray.

Needles of fear swept through my body.

"Seth and Kathleen, you let that homework go," ordered Aunt Phyllis. "We'll do double time next Thursday, but right now we're going to the source!"

Source?

Oh, my.

Aunt Phyllis nearly dragged poor Great-Gramps to the barn to locate the revolting Stock Dip #70 that killed every parasite known to man and beast. Flea and tick soap were like cold cream by comparison.

My stomach curdled at the thought.

Poor little Ms. Margarette was first. How could she know to run? Aunt Phyllis pulled out the big steel tub from behind the toolshed, and Seth filled it with fresh water.

I had only one chance, and that was to hide, but before I could escape into the bushes, Aunt Phyllis had grabbed my collar and was pushing me into the utility room off the kitchen.

"Not so fast, buster," she said. I was instantly intimidated.

I could tell Great-Gramps had no stomach for this kind of cleanliness either. Since he still had stitches on his hand, he excused himself.

"Best I be takin' my nap," he muttered, hanging in the background behind the screen door. He almost got away without being assigned any chores, but Aunt Phyllis stopped him as he headed toward the kitchen.

"Applesauce should be just about right. Give it a stir, add a handful of red-hots, and find some containers. I've got enough to handle right now," she said, going back out to the toolshed. I could watch everything through the screen door. Ms. Margarette wrinkled her nose at first —the smell was quite awful, but with Seth pouring steady fresh water into the tub to protect her young skin, she had a bit of fun, too.

I couldn't watch. I knew my skin would itch for days, and I didn't want to think about it.

Through the door to the kitchen, I could see Great-Gramps at the stove, stirring and counting red-hots. He put in one handful, then another. He tasted the applesauce, then dumped the whole bag of red-hots into the pot.

He made a lot of noise banging cabinet doors as he looked for containers. He kept slipping on the still-damp floor.

He stopped suddenly, remembering something. Then he headed toward the trapdoor near me that led to the cellar below the utility room.

The trapdoor was under a green handmade rug that had a magazine rack on top of it. The rack was there so that people walking through the room wouldn't weaken the flat hatchway. Great-Gramps moved the rack to one side, grabbed a flashlight, and started down to the cellar.

Damp, musty air filled the little room.

I hoped it would disappear before Aunt Phyllis noticed, or there might be another work party next Thursday.

Great-Gramps pulled the hatch closed behind him. That made sense since Maura and little Annie could fall through the opening.

When Aunt Phyllis came in for me, I'm afraid I showed my most cowardly side. She had to drag me.

The little green rug rolled along under my hip and caught in the screen door.

"Honestly, Judge Benjamin, you'll thank me for this later."

I didn't think so.

Aunt Phyllis noticed the green rug, picked it up, and put it back over the hatch. She started to leave, looked behind her, sensed something wasn't quite right, and moved a heavy steel milk can over the rug.

Uh-oh.

Before Great-Gramps could come back up, she was off to drown my fleas, imaginary and otherwise.

I wanted to tell her. I barked, but that made her more determined to scrub. "Sit still, Judge, you don't fool me with that bark."

I tried to go back to the porch to show her.

"You'll not get out of this tub, and that's that!"

No one could call Aunt Phyllis the weaker sex.

The agony of the Stock Dip #70 lasted just a few minutes, but the humiliation didn't stop there. Because I had been an unwilling victim, Aunt Phyllis decided to tie me to the elm tree to make sure I dried without further mischief. Ms. Margarette was tied right beside me. She fell asleep watching the sparrows.

For two hours, I listened to the sounds of the first-floor sterilization. If a flea had any inclinations to remain as a boarder, it had to fight Aunt Phyllis and her crew first.

One thing I didn't hear was Great-Gramps. No pounding, no calling, no nothing.

I heard Aunt Phyllis yell from the kitchen once. "Why didn't somebody turn off this ap-

plesauce?" She put a special emphasis on the word *somebody*, assuming Great-Gramps just forgot on his way to take a nap.

Finally, Maggie came home.

The farmhouse was spotless, and she was thrilled. When she heard about the flea dousing, she came back and unhooked Ms. Margarette and me, whispering, "We better give you a bit of talc to cover that sharp smell." Then she hugged and thanked Aunt Phyllis, who got into her Rolls without changing back into her street clothes.

The car wash attendant would love her designer ensemble.

"Where's Great-Gramps?" Maggie asked.

"Avoiding the work. He took off somewhere for a nap. He doesn't care a hoot about housekeeping, that's for sure." Aunt Phyllis left, but a few feet down the driveway she stopped and threw the Rolls into reverse. She backed up and spoke to Maggie one more time. "Oh, say, I couldn't find any containers for that applesauce."

"Lula always used to keep a good supply of Mason jars in the cellar," Maggie answered, waving good-bye again. "I'll take care of it. You've done quite enough!"

We went into the house through the utility

room, and Maggie, slightly puzzled by the huge milk can in the wrong place, shoved it aside, along with the rug, and pulled the hatch open.

Great-Gramps was sitting cross-legged on the third step, reading a twenty-year-old *Farmer's Almanac* by flashlight. An assortment of Mason jars lined the step above him. He cleared his throat and smiled.

"Great-Gramps! What are you doing here?" Maggie wanted to know.

"Don't tell me. Aunt Phyllis found a tick in my overalls, and it's my turn. . . ." Great-Gramps said in deadpan.

Maggie appeared somewhat confused, but the children were smiling.

"She just left," Maggie said.

When Great-Gramps realized that Aunt Phyllis had indeed left, his sigh of relief was sincere.

Chapter 12

It was the most spectacular Indian summer I had ever seen. The sunrises and sunsets, with all the grounds to explore and enjoy . . . it wasn't home but it was good. When the calendar began to move closer to Halloween, I realized we would be going back to Decatur soon.

Great-Gramps was getting around quite well. After the Demonstration of the Cow Day, he and Ms. Margarette went with Maggie to round up the cows each milking time.

I wondered what it was about Ms. Margarette that made her so good with the farm animals. Her instinct for knowing which way a cow was going to balk even before the cow did was uncanny. Great-Gramps was really proud of her.

Partly because we would be leaving soon, and partly because it was Halloween, Maggie made special plans for celebrating the holiday at Grammy and Pa's house in Metropolis. It was just a half-hour's drive to town.

"Town" wasn't exactly a big city like Decatur. We saw most of it driving down Market Street. There were three drugstores: one had a soda fountain, one was in the building adjoining Farley's Cafeteria, and one was Pa's. Maggie and Tom took the kids and Great-Gramps into Pa's pharmacy to look around and to tell Pa that they would see him at home later.

Ms. Margarette was snoozing, so I stayed in the car with her and watched the people.

I liked Metropolis. Nearly everyone spoke to me as they walked by. There were no parking meters and, of course, no meter maids giving tickets.

Nice.

Because it was Halloween, a big crowd had been drawn to the dime store in the next block. Kids barely made it out the door before emptying their brown sacks and trying on their masks for the night's festivities. One store had a large bin of trick-or-treat candy out front with a sign that said "Treat Yourself."

I watched several children help themselves and was glad to note that none of them took more than two pieces.

I had a feeling that trick-or-treating in Metropolis would be safer and more fun than in Decatur.

When we got to Grammy's house, we were greeted by paper pumpkins and black cats that Grammy had hung inside the screened-in porch.

Grammy answered the door wearing a witch's hat, a silly nose, and plastic glasses. "Happy Halloween, kids," she said, doffing her hat.

Ms. Margarette hesitated when she saw the disguise.

"Is all right, Margrit. Dis is a good widge." Annie scooped up the spooked puppy and carried her into the house.

Seth and Kathleen headed straight for the kitchen, where a big plate of warm pumpkin cookies begged for attention.

"Don't spoil your supper, kids," Maggie warned. "You'll be getting lots more sweets tonight."

I hadn't had a whole lot of experience in the Halloween department—in Decatur it was limited to the neighborhood—but I had a feeling in Metropolis it was going to be my thing. A batch

of caramel apples was hiding behind the toaster,
and I counted three bags of Butterfingers in a
bowl on the dining room table.

"We'll be serving hot chocolate at church
when you trick-or-treaters get tired of combing
the streets tonight," Grammy was saying. "Anyone who wears a costume is welcome. The good-
ies are free."

Costumes? Well, with a face like mine, I
wouldn't need a mask.

"Did you bring the trunk of old clothes down,
or are we going up to the attic?" Maggie asked.

Tom had discovered the Butterfingers. He had
two before Maggie noticed.

Tom groaned. "Oh, I hope you didn't try to
bring the trunk down yourself."

"Of course not," Grammy answered. "That
would mean you'd have to carry it back up later
on, and I'm not that much of a meanie."

Great-Gramps poured some milk for the children and helped himself to a cookie. He handed
one to me and gave a small taste of his to Ms.
Margarette.

She sat on his shoe and waited for more.

"It's fun to go in the attic anyway," Kathleen
said. "Some of those pictures of Mom are so
funny."

"Yeah, remember the one where she was real skinny and her hair was in a ponytail and she had on that long skirt with those funny socks. . . ." Seth was stopped by a pumpkin cookie that Tom thrust quickly into his son's open mouth.

Maggie pretended not to have heard.

"Duz ebryone hab to hab a costoon?" Annie wanted to know.

"Oh, sure," Grammy said. "That's part of the fun."

"Ebryone?" Annie asked again.

"Well, everyone that wants to eat the treats."

I saw Tom roll his eyes heavenward. He knew he'd have to wear a costume, too. All Grammy could do was laugh some more.

Annie was quiet and thoughtful. Then she noticed Henry's empty bed behind the pantry door and tried a new subject. "Where's Henny?"

Maura, who'd been put on the floor, was assembling various old bones from under Henry's bed pillow.

Henry wasn't going to "lub" it.

"Oh, he's hiding under Pa's chair—pouting. I was in a hurry to get the kitchen tidied up before you got here, so I didn't have time to let him lick the cookie pan. Henry's not into forgiving and forgetting," Grammy explained.

I looked through the hall into the living room. A familiar black tail was sticking out under the green rocker. Annie picked up Ms. Margarette and went to try to coax him out.

Nothing doing. That Henry could hold a grudge.

Ms. Margarette heard a muffled growl and jumped out of Annie's arms. She headed back to the security of Great-Gramps's shoe.

Ms. Margarette preferred dealing with quiet cows.

Annie studied Henry for another minute, then looked back at the plate of cookies in the kitchen. "Okay for you, Henny. *I'm* going to hab some cookies."

Henry's tail wagged a bit, and I thought he'd follow. But I guess he hadn't been begged enough.

Tom was opening a Butterfinger, which was a lot more appealing to Annie and me than making friends with that aristocrat.

I bargained for two Butterfingers and got a bonus pumpkin cookie besides.

Chapter 13

We finished our snack, and Grammy started for the attic.

Annie was first in line.

I tried to sneak into second place.

I sucked in my stomach and scrunched low.

"Judge, it's a pretty small attic." Tom was tapping his foot.

I didn't want to miss the fun of an O'Riley trunk showing.

I extended my paw with a gesture that meant "Please."

"I'll stay behind with Maura," Great-Gramps said. "That is, if Annie can find something for me to wear without my help."

Good old Great-Gramps. He patted me on the head, and Tom gave in and let me join the line.

Ms. Margarette was right behind me.

The final flight of stairs was very narrow, but we all squeezed through. The door jammed just as we reached the attic. It must have been painted shut once, and the rain had caused it to swell.

I gave it a good shove, and it opened.

Tom seemed glad I'd come along. Better my paw than his shoulder. He patted my neck.

It was dusty and hot, and there were cobwebs everywhere. Maggie picked up a golf club from behind the door and knocked enough cobwebs down so that we had a passageway.

Tom was too tall to stand up straight, so he blew the dust off an old rocker and sat down.

He had the right idea.

A rag rug was bunched up behind the chair, and I pulled it out and sat down, too.

Ms. Margarette found a basket with scraps of material and began teething on a long piece of gray wool. She got pretty aggressive and, with one good head shake, managed to dislodge a mirror standing behind the basket. It slid down flat on the floor but didn't break.

She heard the noise behind her and jumped.

One rear paw landed on the mirror, which probably felt cold and not as soft as all those material scraps. When she turned to investigate, she saw a springer spaniel puppy with some gray wool hanging out of its mouth.

Ms. Margarette barked and dropped the wool.

Amazing. So did the other spaniel.

She took a couple of cautious steps onto the mirror.

Oh, boy. More of the spaniel.

Tom and I were both getting a kick out of her first encounter with her own reflection. I began wagging my tail.

It wasn't wise.

There was a sharp sting at the end of it and a loud popping noise that sounded like a cap gun.

Tom laughed. "Couldn't resist the cheese, huh, Judge?"

He reached over to pull off a mousetrap.

Thank goodness. I thought I'd been shot.

"Better be careful," he said, rubbing the sore spot. "This place is mined."

Well, better my tail than Ms. Margarette's nose.

We heard a scratching noise coming up the steps. I thought we might be getting one of those mice Grammy expected.

But it was a bigger, blacker tail that scooted into the attic. Henry's.

He was licking his face, and he smelled a lot like pumpkin cookies.

Henry marched up close enough to the mirror for his nose to be reflected at one end, and Ms. Margarette thought her spaniel was being attacked.

Her little bark really got going.

"Hey, you guys, if you don't settle down, this attic won't be big enough for all of us," Maggie said sternly, looking at the four-legged offenders.

Ms. Margarette hated to be scolded. She disappeared behind a big orange box filled with newspapers. When Maggie turned back to the trunk, Ms. Margarette came out with layers of cobwebs on her nose and newsprint on her white chest.

Henry harrumphed his way to another rug.

We watched the whole family, digging and rummaging in trunks and suitcases and boxes. In short order there was a costume for everybody —even an artist's outfit for Great-Gramps. Little Annie, who had put together all that was necessary to be "Little Pink Riding Hood," was the only one still fumbling for props.

"I need a basgit for goodees for Grammy—like in the story," Annie decided. She spotted the

one with the material scraps, dumped them un-ceremoniously on the floor, and waved the basket in the air.

"Dis'll be fine," she said.

Ms. Margarette, who had been watching the whole episode, tumbled into the scrap pile. Just as Annie set the basket down again, Ms. Margarette jumped inside of it with a mouthful of scraps.

"Okay, Ms. Margrit. You be lunch." With that, Annie picked up a strange-looking bonnet that was covered with plastic fruit decorations and stuck it on Ms. Margarette's head.

"Ms. Margarette!" Maggie removed the hat and pulled her out of the basket. "Sorry. Halloween isn't for dogs."

Annie was aghast. "It isn't? Why not?"

"Well, it just isn't, honey." Maggie was aware that she had backed herself into a toddler-parent-no-win debate. After all, even Great-Gramps was going to take part.

I could read the handwriting on the wall.

"Grammy, you said ebryone wid a costoon could trick-or-treat."

"Well, yes, dear, but I meant . . ." Grammy was at a loss for an argument.

"Look, Annie, if you carry Ms. Margarette in

that basket, how are you going to carry the treats you get?" It was Seth making a stab at his best big-brother argument.

"Judge'll hep me," Annie said.

Oh, dear.

"Wait a minute, Annie. You mean you want all three dogs to march on the great Halloween candy walk?" Kathleen buried her head in a printed skirt to hide a laugh.

Annie was *so* sincere.

"'Course."

"Won't work," Kathleen finally managed to say. "You might be able to drag Ms. Margarette along like a ham sandwich, but no one will ever convince Henry that he has to dress up to get his share of candy."

"I will. I will so. We'll make him . . . we'll make him . . ."

As Seth started picking up the material scraps from the floor, he ran across a long strand of blue polished cotton. "I know," he said, draping the ribbon across Henry's shoulder and chest, "we'll just write *Miss America* on this."

I was going to be sick.

"Annie, I just don't think Henry will . . ." Grammy was still trying to think of a reason that a very little girl could understand. Only Henry, true to form, decided to make everyone look dumb. He pranced around the attic, puffing out his chest and looking for all the world like a contestant for the Miss America pageant.

I wasn't sure things were going in my favor. I had an uncomfortable feeling that my dignity was about to become meat loaf.

Seth was holding up an old black cap and gown. "Was this Mom's?" he asked.

"No," Maggie said. "That was Pa's from pharmacy school."

Seth was approaching me. I tried to fade into the floor. "Hey, Judge, wanna be a graduate?"

He threw the robe around my shoulders.

Tom helped him arrange it with folds and pins. "I don't know what kind of degree they'd give a two-hundred-pound St. Bernard. Doctor of Dog Biscuits?" he said.

Seth struggled with the mortarboard. It was much too tight, and it kept slipping down my ear.

Kathleen's head popped out of the bottom of the trunk. "Wait. I've got a better idea!" She was holding a white George Washington wig. "We'll make the Judge a judge!"

I couldn't go anywhere. The attic was too small. So I sat still and hoped they would all change their mind.

"It'll be fun, Judge," Annie said.

I could see my reflection out of the corner of my eye in Ms. Margarette's mirror.

This was justice?

"You know something, Judge? I kind of like the idea," Maggie said. "If you went along, I wouldn't worry about the kids."

That was it, I guess. I'd be going in the line of duty.

By the time we left the attic, I'd accepted the dress code. Even though the whole family would be going to the party at church, the house-to-house candy grab was to be just children and dogs. It was my rightful place. I wasn't crazy about the dumb costume, but Annie was so thrilled, and well, sometimes it pays to swallow one's pride.

Great-Gramps dressed up early so he could answer the door bell in style. Maggie cut a pallette-shaped cardboard for him which he clamped in his "magic" hand. He stuck a paintbrush over his ear and put on a beret. Just to give the right touch, he spotted his face with dabs of various watercolors, and painted a mustache above his mouth. His smock and pants were smeared with paint, too.

If there was a better example in the good-sport department, I didn't know who it would be.

When the door bell rang, Great-Gramps balanced apples on his pallette, raised it over his head, and bowed—very slowly and *very* carefully.

The trick-or-treaters loved it.

As the rest of us got ready to set off, Annie dressed Ms. Margarette up to ride in comfort. Annie tied a soft white baby bonnet on Ms. Margarette's head and tucked her into the basket with a white receiving blanket and a white pillow. It wasn't the lunch described in the original Red Riding Hood story, but Annie was quite satisfied. With all that white, Ms. Margarette looked more like a ghost than a baby.

Like any good baby, Ms. Margarette promptly went to sleep.

Kathleen spent some time making a foil crown for Henry, but he kept trying to eat it.

It was a powerful "nothin' doin'," so Kathleen gave up on that.

Kathleen was hard to identify in her cowboy ghost costume, and Seth looked pretty funny in his garden-girl setup. He drew the line when Maggie tried to curl his hair, but he was cheerful enough to pose for pictures.

I tried to feel the spirit of things.

Pa and Grammy took turns with the camera so

everyone could have a record of their getups.

Grammy kept talking about future generations.

All I could think of was living through the night.

Chapter 14

Finally, we were off.

My wig itched, but I didn't dare scratch it.

Kathleen had tied it to my collar so it wouldn't slip around. I knew I'd end up choking myself if I tried to tug at it.

Fortunately, a brisk wind lifted it just enough to give me some relief now and then.

Henry led the way.

I knew he would.

He should have been mayor.

He barked at everyone and everything. We could hardly call him an elegant leader, but he did clear the sidewalk for us.

Nearly every house was lighted and decorated for Halloween. Annie followed the traditional "trick-or-treat" example of her brother and sister at the first two houses, but altered her approach when she examined the terrific sweets that people put in her bag. Before the end of the first block, she was racing ahead with her bag open, simply shouting, "Candeeees! Candeeees?"

That worked, too.

It was really kind of fun. Metropolitans were friendly and cheerful, and they almost always slipped something to me, too.

Mrs. Gillespie had the most mouth-watering popcorn ball I ever sunk my teeth into. She gave an extra one to Kathleen to save for that "big funny dog" later.

Since Grammy and Pa knew everyone within walking distance of their house, there were no strangers to worry about.

It was smooth going.

I should have known it couldn't last.

It started to crumble at the house with the caramels. Dr. and Mrs. Green had made a batch of homemade sugarless caramels as a personal campaign to hold down tooth decay. But sugarless caramels have a tendency to be gritty, and I wasn't prepared for my mouthful.

While I was struggling with my bound molars,

Henry was flirting with the Fraziers'
Pomeranian, who was swinging on her own pink
glider on the Fraziers' porch across the street.

Then there was the problem of Kathleen's
cowboy boots. She had chosen them as an after-
thought, and she should have thought further.
They were too big and stiff, and the insoles were
peeling. She had to keep stopping to readjust
them.

Seth's hat met with a gust of wind, and he, too,
fell behind.

But Annie, with her goody baby basket, kept
charging ahead.

The fire engine was the last straw. It had taken
off down Girard Street when a call came in about
a small jack-o'-lantern falling into a pile of leaves.
When the truck got to the block we were travel-
ing, the piercing siren woke Ms. Margarette.

Her little black nose peeked out of the basket.
She saw the streak of red, heard the noise, and
bolted.

That fire engine was no cow, and that siren
was no moo.

Ms. Margarette landed in a somersault and
took off running. Her receiving blanket caught
on the tie of her bonnet and dragged along behind her.

Kathleen was still having trouble with her oversized boots and had taken them off, trying to figure out a more permanent solution. She didn't see Ms. Margarette jump.

Seth tried to catch Ms. Margarette, but he kept tripping on his skirt.

Annie ran as far as the street corner, remembered she wasn't allowed to cross alone, and stopped dead in her tracks.

The chase was on.

I couldn't even bark since my mouth was glued shut with those chewy treats. Henry, still batting his eyes at the Pomeranian chickadee, couldn't have cared less.

The poor little dog was getting snowed.

Foolish femme.

Other cars followed the fire engine. Some were filled with volunteers, and others held only spectators, but the screeching of tires continued. Ms. Margarette really got spooked. Lights, squeals, shadows—it was a miracle no car hit her.

She just kept running.

The brisk wind behind her pushed her along faster and faster.

My robe had come unpinned over my right leg, and I was tripping just like Seth.

Ms. Margarette headed toward the Ohio

River, four blocks south of Grammy's house. It was high and rough, as always in the fall.

All along the way she kept dodging other trick-or-treaters.

I watched the wind pick her clear up off the ground a couple of times, her blanket and bonnet serving as a kind of sail. When she landed, the combination of blanket and bonnet worked more like a parachute.

Ms. Margarette passed the last street before the river. I breathed a sigh of relief that there'd be no more cars to threaten her.

She was heading for the grove of trees the Junior Welfare had planted years before to hold back the eroding bank. The wind was swirling around the nearly leafless branches and was picking up strength from the water.

I was finally closing in on the little ghost on the run when the wind played its trump card.

Ms. Margarette rose, higher this time, the blanket waving and flying . . .

. . . and catching on a branch of the small elm near the picnic table on the bank of the Ohio.

I was afraid she'd be strangled, or worse, be thrust to the ground by another gust.

Her little paws circled a branch, and there she stayed, howling and crying like a stray cat.

I jumped on the picnic table to try to pull her free.

That's when the police car that patrolled the river made its move.

Maybe the policeman suspected vandals. I'm not sure what he thought. But when he came closer, he could see a baby ghost with a black nose and a white furry chest and a Judge with an incredibly handsome face attacking park property.

In the dark of the night with the shadows that were created by the full moon behind us, even innocence would have to be misunderstood.

That wasn't the worst of it.

It was then that dear heroic Casanova Henry tore himself from his merrymaking and joined the party.

Not having witnessed the whole adventure, he saw only a crying Ms. Margarette and a policeman with a big club advancing on his friends.

He growled ferociously, yelped, and pounced.

Henry bit the policeman's shoe.

Kathleen, Seth, and Annie arrived soon enough to mention the magic names of Grammy and Pa, so we didn't have to go to the police station. But we did ride home in the police car: a country girl with short hair and freckles, a limping western Casper, Little Pink Riding Hood, Miss America, Judge Benjamin, and baby Margarette, who promptly fell asleep with the motion of the squad car.

When we pulled up to number 409, the policeman also saw a small group making their way down the front porch to the church party. There was a witch in a swishing taffeta skirt, her arms around a huge sheet cake; a lady gangster in a pin-striped suit with a red carnation, balancing two jugs of cider; a middle-aged Superman hoisting a baby on his shoulders; a senior citizen posing as Picasso; and a Musketeer with silk breeches and gray hair peeking out below his three-cornered hat as he locked the front door.

I wish we could have followed that policeman home to hear the story he told his wife.

Chapter 15

Grammy shouldn't have worried about preserving pictures for future generations.

When we arrived at the Church Hall for the party, Father Jerry met us at the door wearing Mickey Mouse ears and short pants. He introduced us immediately to the newspaperman with the camera who flashed bulbs in between laughter.

Making the weekly *Metropolis News* was big time.

Ms. Margarette, awed a bit by all the attention and the people, kept hiding under Kathleen's skirt. That is, until Mr. and Mrs. McCoglin came in a cow costume and she followed the plastic tail. She was confused, but she kept them under thoughtful surveillance for the rest of the night.

Henry found a spot under the buffet table very near the pecan tarts. He sat looking soulful so that people would slip him some.

Nearly everyone did.

He was going to have one heck of a bellyache.

When Annie fell asleep on my paws and Maura started crying for that bedtime bottle, we went back to Grammy's house.

The kids were worn out, and so was I.

Tom would be heading out of town early the next morning to make a three-day visit to Waterloo again, and since Great-Gramps was so much better, Maggie and the kids were going to stay in Metropolis. Tom would drop Great-Gramps off at the farm on his way out of town in the morning. Great-Gramps would be in charge of the cows for the early milking.

The rest of the family would join him later in the day.

We weren't going to be needed much longer.

Maybe that's why I woke early when Tom and Great-Gramps were catching a cup of coffee before they left. Well, that and Henry's snoring. I never could sleep late with that guy in the next room.

Kathleen was up, too. Ms. Margarette had pouted and paced until she was allowed to sleep near the door on the porch, so Kathleen had slept on the glider to periodically calm her.

It was out of character for Ms. Margarette to be so restless, but she missed her cows. Ever since she'd found the "just this once" sleeping spot in the front of the barn, she grew restless any place else.

When Tom and Great-Gramps got in the car, Kathleen was already in the back seat holding Ms. Margarette. "Mom said it was okay. Okay?" Tom nodded.

Kathleen seemed very quiet as we drove to the farm. I knew she had something on her mind.

The wind of the night before had ushered in something of a storm. Big black clouds clumped together in the sky, and I was glad we were keeping Great-Gramps company. Maggie and the others would be joining us soon, but on a dark early morning, the farm seemed a lonely place.

Tom offered to stay, but Great-Gramps wouldn't think of it. "With all this help?" Great-Gramps joked, pointing to Kathleen, Ms. Margarette, and me.

"Don't worry, Dad. We can handle it," Kathleen said.

By the time the milking was done, the rumble of thunder was loud and close. A fast rain shooed us inside the house.

Kathleen made tea and cinnamon toast. The four of us, Ms. Margarette cuddled on Kathleen's lap, sat on the porch to watch the storm.

"Looks like a humdinger," Great-Gramps said softly.

A boom of thunder made us all jump.

"Don't you get scared sometimes, all alone?" Kathleen asked.

"I don't think about it much," Great-Gramps replied.

"I do. I don't like to be alone," Kathleen said.

"Maybe that's because you so seldom are." Great-Gramps reached for another piece of toast.

He gave it to me.

I was very glad Kathleen had made plenty.

Kathleen started to ask another question but stopped herself. She was holding Ms. Margarette very firmly and was deep in thought.

We sat there listening to the sounds of the storm and watching the lightning that was streaking closer now.

"Glad we got the animals in 'fore it rained," Great-Gramps said. "They get confused with the weather sometimes."

The lightning became horizontal—big, bold lines as bright as sunlight.

I wondered if anyone else's heart was beating faster than mine.

Great-Gramps stood up. "That one was pretty close to that old silo. I don't like it."

I seldom heard Great-Gramps worry about anything, and it made me nervous.

Pretty soon we were all standing at the rail, drawn to those crazy streaks of light as if they were trying to tell us something.

"Great-Gramps! *The barn!* It hit the barn!" Kathleen didn't have to say it. We all saw it. We all felt the same hard twinge. The dry hay, the combustible stock dip supply, the old wood—it would go like kindling.

Great-Gramps was already at the back door, grabbing his hat and bandanna. He slid a yellow slicker over his head and yelled back to Kathleen, "Call the fire department—the number's by the phone. I've got to get those animals."

"Great-Gramps, you can't!" Kathleen grabbed his arm.

"I have no choice. Horses won't leave a burning barn. It's their home. And it's my job."

I didn't know what good I could do, but I ran with him.

The rain was hard now. It was tough even to see. But it was the only thing that slowed the fire.

There was so much that could burn and burn quickly. Great-Gramps raced through the barn, opening the stalls of the horses and cows. But they didn't move.

We went for the horses first. He wrapped the bandanna over one mare's eyes and threw me a rope from around her neck. *"Pull,* Judge. Get her out of here."

He was already at the next stall, tying an old towel around the second horse's eyes and pulling it out of the stall himself.

Those horses weren't exactly willing. Only when they couldn't see the fire could they be convinced to leave their burning home.

There were still two more to go, and none of the cows were out.

Kathleen was running up, little Ms. Margarette right behind her.

Great-Gramps threw the horses' lead ropes to her. "Tie these mares to the wagon up by the fence, Kathleen," he yelled.

There wasn't time to argue.

We went back in, the smoke stinging my eyes. We got the other two horses, the fire closing around us, the heat burning my chest.

I don't know how we made it out. A beam fell just inches from my paw, and I felt the sizzle of fur. Great-Gramps smothered it, and we kept going.

But the cows. We couldn't get to them. The smoke held us back like a brick wall and confused the cows so that they couldn't find their own way out.

The last horse got wild with the heat and kicked and bucked until his hooves had booted the big barn door closed again.

When we tried to open it, the heat had fused it shut.

Our strength was gone.

Great-Gramps sat on the ground puffing and coughing.

I felt so bad for him. At least the horses were safe.

Ms. Margarette danced at the door, barking and angry. *Her cows.*

I underestimated her sense of duty. She didn't just bark.

She went into that burning barn through the opening at the bottom that had been her sleeping spot.

Kathleen screamed.

She clenched her fists, bit her lip in a hard, fast prayer, and then yelled, "The ropes, we'll get the ropes."

Great-Gramps rose with his last ounce of strength. Kathleen had already slipped the ropes off of two horses and tied them to the crossbar on the barn door. "We've got to pull, we've all got to pull." She tied one end of the rope under my chest, and she and Great-Gramps yanked at the other.

I don't know how we managed it—Great-Gramps and I were so spent—but in that magic moment when adrenaline rises to incredible need, we pulled the barn door open again.

That's when we heard it.

Bossy Lou's bell.

Not one ring, but many—*clang*, then *clang* again.

A black-and-white pup was jumping and ringing Bossy Lou's bell.

The other cows just followed the sound.

Every single cow was saved.

Chapter 16

It had not been the first fire on Great-Gramps's farm. It was the third. Once a tractor spark had ignited the toolshed. Great-Gramps lost a bundle on uninsured equipment that time. Another year, spontaneous combustion had set off an alarm in one of the unused outbuildings. Great-Gramps and Lula had kept the fire under control with buckets and hoses until the city fire truck could make the eighteen-mile trip to put it out. That fire had come close to spreading to the main house. When it came to accepting a loss, Great-Gramps needed no coaching.

"Nobody was hurt," he answered simply, " 'cept old Judge Benjamin's paw. And he's due for a bit o' rest anyway."

My paw was sore, but it was a small burn. Doc Higgins assured us that the fur would grow back. As far as the family was concerned, the canine population held only heroes.

Make that heroes and heroines. Kathleen told and retold the story of little Ms. Margarette's rescue. Each of us heard it at least three times apiece. At the last count, poor Maura had been subjected to half a dozen versions.

One thing was very clear to all of us—Ms. Margarette believed those cows were hers. She spent more and more time with them.

The biggest problem was rebuilding the barn before winter.

Tom got busy, determined to beat his own production record. Since the Wisconsin job was nearly finished, Tom brought his crew down in the camper to manage the barn rebuilding. I don't know how he got the materials delivered so fast, but there they were, his men, some of Pa's friends from town, and the family, pounding, laughing, hoisting beams, laying tarp, then shingles. It was completed in a record three days.

We were sitting in the wagon, the big one for hay hauling that was parked by the fence, watching the last of the barn-red paint going on.

Great-Gramps had taken Ms. Margarette with

him to the milk house for the evening job.

"Something isn't exactly right," Kathleen said softly.

"Not exactly right! It's a perfect job!" Tom said, laughing.

Kathleen jumped down from the wagon and walked to the big door. "No, it's not the same."

Seth got down and stood with his sister. "She's right. I see a problem."

Tom put Maura on his shoulders and walked up with Maggie. I think they knew what Kathleen was driving at, but they decided to let her finish it her own way.

"Oopsie, I know." Annie said running up. "You blocked up Margrit's house!"

"Is that the problem, Kathleen?" Tom asked. He somehow felt the answer should come from her.

I think she was trying not to cry.

"Yes, Dad. This is Ms. Margarette's home, too."

Seth was already piling some shingles to one side. "What we ought to do, Dad . . ."

They did what they thought they ought to do. Tom cut a small rectangular opening on one side of the barn door. He nailed down tarp strips for protection against bad weather but still made it open enough for Ms. Margarette to come and go. Just above the opening, Seth nailed a small roof, an angle of shingles that marked her spot.

Maura and Annie wanted to help, so Maggie found some morning glory seeds in Lula's "everything" drawer and we planted them on either side of Ms. Margarette's door.

Kathleen found white paint, and stenciled letters onto a sign above the mock roof.

Ms. MARGARETTE . . .

. . . COWDOG.

When the suitcases were loaded in the car and we stood on the porch to say good-bye, Kathleen

brought Great-Gramps and Ms. Margarette down to the barn.

Kathleen picked up the puppy and handed her to Great-Gramps. "You'd better take care of each other," she said. "Ms. Margarette has agreed to tell me everything."

The moment could have been awkward—I expected to see tears in Kathleen's eyes.

But it wasn't that way. She rubbed Ms. Margarette's ears and kissed Great-Gramps's cheek. Everyone else got in the hugging-and-kissing act then. When we were all in the car, Annie ran out one more time to squeeze Great-Gramps's knee —it was the easiest thing to reach.

Great-Gramps walked over to Kathleen's window. "You don't have to look behind you to know your shadow's there, Kathleen," he said. "Even if you don't see it, it's part of you." He patted her hand and walked slowly back to the porch, Ms. Margarette at his heels.

We were on our way.

It might have been a sad trip, but Annie broke the ice. "I got an idee. Judge Benjamin can hab puppies!"

Everyone laughed.

Seth explained. "Boy dogs can't have puppies, Annie. You know that."

Annie wouldn't give up. "He can do ebryting else."

Sweet Annie—but there are some miracles even she can't muster.

Kathleen changed the subject. "I wonder who won the spelling bees," she said.

"Will Sister Mary Clare make us take the six-weeks exams without review?" Seth wondered aloud, suddenly aware that he had some catching up to do.

There was a bit of light conversation for a while longer. Then the kids played two games of Twenty Questions before they all dozed off. Maura was the first to close her eyes, and Kathleen was the last.

With the kids asleep, Maggie had changed stations from rock to Bach on the radio.

Maura was purring that soft, gentle snore that babies sound, and from the back window a pattern of lightly falling snow melted as it landed on the road behind us.

Thank goodness the new barn was finished.

We would have to wait till spring to know if Ms. Margarette's morning glories would be blue or white or both. I was hoping for both. She would like that.

It was a new season. Sunshine and shadows

must move on. Soon, very soon, I would be back with my apple trees, meeting school buses, breaking the draft in my spot at the back door.

Kathleen stirred, her arm brushing my bandaged paw. It hardly hurt now.

We would all miss Ms. Margarette.

For that matter, we would all miss Great-Gramps.

But a little part of them would always be a part of us.

My heart was very full.

I couldn't help wondering if anywhere in the whole world there could be another St. Bernard as lucky as me.

ABOUT THE AUTHOR

JUDITH WHITELOCK MCINERNEY grew up in the small town of Metropolis, Illinois, and started her writing career at age seven with the printing of her Brownie Troop minutes in the *Metropolis News*. Eventually she wrote her own column during high school, and went on to graduate from the College of Journalism at Marquette University in Milwaukee, Wisconsin. After marrying her college sweetheart, she had four children, who figure in this novel with their own lovable St. Bernard, Judge Benjamin, as the hero. Her children, three girls and a boy, range in age from kindergarten through high school and are sure to be part of the author's upcoming books. The McInerneys presently make their home in Decatur, Illinois. *Judge Benjamin: Superdog Secret* is available in an Archway Paperback edition.